I0632325

C. B. Howard

Paths that Crossed

glimpses into the early days of Methodism and of Georgia, a centenary tribute

C. B. Howard

Paths that Crossed
glimpses into the early days of Methodism and of Georgia, a centenary tribute

ISBN/EAN: 9783337255800

Printed in Europe, USA, Canada, Australia, Japan

Cover: Foto ©Andreas Hilbeck / pixelio.de

More available books at **www.hansebooks.com**

PATHS THAT CROSSED:

OR

GLIMPSES INTO THE EARLY DAYS OF METHODISM AND OF GEORGIA.

—

A CENTENARY TRIBUTE.

—

BY MRS. C. B. HOWARD.
ATLANTA, GA.

—

"In all thy ways acknowledge him, and he shall direct thy paths."
Proverbs iii. 6.

NASHVILLE, TENN.:
SOUTHERN METHODIST PUBLISHING HOUSE.
1885.

Entered, according to Act of Congress, in the year 1885,
BY THE BOOK AGENTS OF THE METHODIST EPISCOPAL CHURCH, SOUTH,
in the Office of the Librarian of Congress, at Washington.

PREFACE.

HISTORIES of Methodism and of Georgia are many and complete. This little volume does not aspire to that dignity; it is simply a Centenary offering—glimpses here and there, as the title indicates, of "crossing paths" that made life better and happier for those who met. The author sincerely hopes that this warp of fiction, almost hidden by the woof of truth, of fact, and of sound doctrine, will render the finished web interesting and helpful to those who read; so, in *her path* thus crossing theirs, may she fulfill one great desire of her life—to be a "fellow-helper to the truth."

Acknowledgments of assistance are gratefully made to the following works: "Life of John Wesley," by the Rev. Luke Tyerman; "History of Georgia," by Col. C. C. Jones, jr.; "Wesley Memorial Volume," by Dr. J. O. A. Clarke; "The Women of Methodism," by Dr. Abel Stevens.

To My Venerable Father,

MAJOR FRANCIS R. SHACKELFORD,

Who, in His Eighty-fourth Year, Distinctly Remem-
bers the Pioneer Bishop Asbury, Whose Hands
were Placed in Blessing on His Head,

and

Whose Admiration and Love for Mr. Wesley
Know No Bounds,

THESE PAGES ARE INSCRIBED.

PATHS THAT CROSSED;

OR,

GLIMPSES INTO THE EARLY DAYS OF METHODISM AND OF GEORGIA.

N the beginning God created the heaven and the earth. . . He made the stars also. . And God set them in the firmament of the heaven. . . And God saw that it was good." Then " the morning-stars sung together, and all the sons of God shouted for joy." Then were unbound "the sweet influences of Pleiades;" then were unloosed the "bands of Orion;" then was "Mazzaroth brought forth in his season;" and then began the guidance of "Arcturus with his sons."

Untold ages have passed since were given "the ordinances of the moon and of the stars," and still they pursue their trackless course in the circuit of heaven as undeviatingly as they did in the early dawn of creation.

With wondering awe and admiration, doubtless, did our first parents gaze upon them, with

hearts unconscious of sin, and all aglow with
love and gratitude to their Almighty Maker and
Friend.   We can fancy them as, fanned by the per-
fumed breezes of paradise, they sauntered slowly
along the banks of the gently-flowing river that
" went out of Eden," attracting each other's attention first to one and then another of the shining
host above them—the first mortal eyes that had ever
looked upon the glittering throng.

As years passed on, as the lovely garden—ten-
antless—was guarded by the cherubim's flaming
sword, as the children of men increased, and "shep-
herds watched their flocks by night," imagination
can easily depict the interest that gathered around
these heavenly bodies, till in course of time super-
stition and error sought to supply the wisdom that
humanity craved, and astrologers, peering into unknown and hidden things, essayed to taste once
more of the tree of knowledge.

In the clearer light of the later time science has
somewhat pierced into the hitherto great unknown.
The wonderful modern telescope aids us in an attempt to fathom the great abyss of the sidereal
heavens.   An attempt, indeed—for after we have
learned all that its space-penetrating power can
reveal, with giddy brain we cease to compute the
limitless spaces; with failing imagination we turn
from the vast magnitudes; with blinded gaze our
vision wearies of the dazzling works of the Great

Architect; and in breathless humility we bow in adoration, saying, " Great and marvelous are thy works, Lord God Almighty!"

Nor need we fear that the movements of the stellar universe will cease " while the earth remaineth;" for since the " hosts of heaven were made by the breath of His mouth," and swung off, each into his separate orbit, they " continue as they were from the beginning."

There is no mistake or miscalculation in the handiwork of the Omnipotent Engineer. Each in his own particular path pursues his course. To us who gaze upon them, their tracks appear confused, involved, a maze of tangled contradictions, ever risking collision and instant destruction; but He who marks the sparrow's fall is guiding these careering planets. He brings unerring order out of apparent chaos. Their bounds are fixed. With speed more rapid than the lightning's flash, unwearied as an archangel's wing, they fly, fulfilling the behest of their Great Original, and

> Forever singing as they shine,
> "The hand that made us is divine."

Now, while we can unite our *benedicite* with that of the three Hebrew children, and exclaim, "O ye stars of heaven, bless ye the Lord; praise him, and magnify him forever!" surely we should add: "O ye children of men, O ye spirits and souls of the righteous, bless ye the Lord; praise him, and magnify him forever!" For we also "are the works of his hands." Did God make the stars? So, also, did he "create man in his own image, and breathed into his nostrils the breath of life;" therefore this living soul may, amid "the wreck of matter and the crush of worlds,"

> The darkening universe defy
> To quench his immortality,
> Or shake his trust in God;

may, when "the heavens being on fire shall be dissolved, and the elements shall melt with fervent heat," enter into an inheritance "that fadeth not away, reserved in heaven;" for, "he that overcometh, and keepeth my works [saith the Lord] unto the end, to him will I give the morning-star;" for "I Jesus am the bright and morning star."

Shall "blind unbelief, so sure to err, and scan God's works in vain," prompt us to doubt that the same Almighty Hand which guides the stars in their courses shall fail to direct our steps, when we have his promise: "In all thy ways acknowledge him, and he shall direct thy paths?" No, rather let us believe the Scripture, where it is written: "A man's heart deviseth his way, but the Lord directeth his steps."

Not more certainly are the orbits of the stars planned by the All-wise One than are the pathways of them that love God. We may not be able to trace, to unravel, or to understand; but when in the light of eternity all that is dark is made clear, when in the "harbor of God's finished mystery" we anchor, then we shall be *satisfied*. Till then human paths will cross, and the contact will influence souls eternally. Some will impinge with frightful force, and never-ending misery will ensue; others will meet and, mutually blessed, run in parallel lines henceforth; still others will but touch, but the result will be cause of thanksgiving in the courts of heaven.

It is interesting to trace and study these subtle influences as well as our limited opportunity, our immature judgment, and our partial vision allow. In the succeeding pages we wish to follow some " paths that crossed;" to narrate many facts, a few fancies; to describe what certainly took place, and what easily might have been; to make familiar characters and scenes we love to dwell upon, and yet heretofore have not dwelt upon enough. May profit and pleasure attend the perusal.

→CHAPTER I.←

IN the county of Lincoln, England, on the 17th of June, 1703, in a humble village rectory, "a child was born."

Many centuries before, the question had been asked, "What manner of child shall this be?" and the father of John the Baptist, "filled with the Holy Ghost," had prophesied: "And thou, child, shalt be called the prophet of the Highest; for thou shalt go before the face of the Lord to prepare his ways; to give knowledge of salvation unto his people by the remission of their sins, through the tender mercy of our God; whereby the dayspring from on high hath visited us, to give light to them that sit in darkness and in the shadow of death, to guide our feet into the way of peace." The Christ, for whom he had prepared the way, declared: "Among those that are born of women there is not a greater prophet than John the Baptist; but he that is least in the kingdom of God is greater than he."

When the infant of Epworth Rectory was baptized, his father and mother might have asked the question that so stirred the heart of Zacharias—as thousands of godly parents have inquired since that time. Had it been granted to them to look forward through the long stretch of eighty-eight years, and to know what that babe would be and would do for the world and for Christ; had they been able, looking through that long and glorious vista, to see the far prospective of a hundred added years opening up, and heard the name of their son *John Wesley*, upon the tongues and enshrined in the hearts of millions of his fellow-beings, who blessed God that he had lived upon this earth; if (with reverence be it spoken) their earth-beclouded eyes could have had the mists of time swept away, and a glance into the vast eternity vouchsafed them, where among the

"great multitude, which no man could number,
standing before the throne and before the Lamb,"
were myriads who hailed him as the means, under
God, of their present bliss, who were the "stars in
his crown of rejoicing;" had, indeed, this wonderful revelation been granted them, overwhelmed with
gratitude and joy, how, like Mary of old, would
their souls have "magnified their Lord," and how
profoundly would they have recognized the fact that
in their arms they infolded, in their tiny infant they
beheld, one greater than John the Baptist—a prophet of the gospel of the New Testament, a preacher
of the crucified, the risen, the ascended Jesus! But
the vast possibilities of the future were hidden from
their view. To them he seemed, what in fact he
was, but one of their nineteen children. The devoted mother cared for his wants physically, mentally, spiritually, with the same system, wisdom, and
gentle firmness she always observed. It would be
interesting and beneficial, to mothers especially, if,
by some unknown process of mathematics, the extreme advantages of her plan could be figured out.
Management in a family of thirteen children—for
that number were living at one time—that resulted
in order and quiet, where the "odious noise of crying children was rarely heard" after one year of
age, and yet where the little ones were peculiarly
affectionate to each other and devoted to their mother, deserves wide imitation. She taught her chil-

dren regularly for six hours each day. She superintended not only the domestic arrangements of her
household, but the outdoor business of the glebe—
her husband being absorbed in his study. While
teaching her children the magnitude of personal responsibility, she knit their hearts closely together
by a wise arrangement for mutual help and profit,
by which at a stated hour every afternoon the oldest took the youngest that could speak, the second
the next, and so on, to whom they read the Psalm
for the day and a chapter in the New Testament;
supplementing these instructions herself every night
by conversing with one, sometimes with two, of her
children on religious subjects.

What hour and what circumstances can be more
propitious for such tender, heart-searching intercourse with the young immortals intrusted to our
care than the quiet moments when they seek repose?
Then can they be gently led to self-examination, to
repentance, to trust in God; and as with softened
hearts they recognize their mother's earnest solicitude for their spiritual interests, impressions may be
made that will result in abundant fruitage, perchance, when those loving eyes and tender tones are
closed and hushed in death.

Still more, Mrs. Wesley, amid the numerous cares
and demands upon her time, which would seem almost to absorb it, appeared to appreciate the truth
of this statement: "If you would do all your duty

to your children, learn all you can of God's word, and in your experience realize all you can of God's grace."* In furtherance of such an object, she reserved to herself one hour every morning and evening, where in entire seclusion she could devote herself to meditation and prayer.

Where wealth with its accompaniments of leisure and opportunity are granted, such fine results as this admirable mother achieved may not occasion surprise; but her circumstances were straitened almost to suffering. For many years two hundred and fifty dollars had to supply food and raiment, and at their best estate one thousand dollars per annum was their entire fortune. So pressed with poverty and oftentimes with debt, we gaze with admiration at the more than fortitude, the Christian philosophy, that enabled this noble woman to preserve a cheerful equanimity at all times; not only performing faithfully her duty to her children and her household, but during her husband's enforced absence reading sermons, praying and conversing, in her own house, with the assembled rustics of his parish. Reading her life, which every mother may do with profit, well may we indorse the commendation bestowed upon her by Dr. Adam Clarke, who writes: "Such a woman, take her for all in all, I have not heard of, I have not read of, nor with her equal have I been acquainted. Such a one Solo-

* Dr. A. G. Haygood.

mon has described in the last chapter of his Proverbs; and to her I can apply the summed-up character of his accomplished housewife: 'Many daughters have done virtuously, but Susanna Wesley has
excelled them all.'"

Nor need we suppose that Epworth Rectory was
an austere home, where the merry exuberance of
childhood was repressed and their lives set to the
measured music of the gravity and experience of
tempered age. So far from it, that we read although method and system were observed with almost mechanical rigor, yet in spite of this—shall
we not say *because* of it?—the relaxation at suitable
intervals converted the nursery into an " arena of
hilarious recreations, of high glee and frolic; games
of skill and even chance being among the family
pastimes;" wit and humor being characteristics of
almost each member of the circle, who "had the
common fame of being the most loving family in
the county of Lincoln; the mother especially being the center of the household affections."

And so the quiet years rolled on, till one night
when this child, whose name, the past has proved,
"was not born to die," was suddenly seized between
the very jaws of death, and narrowly escaped un-
hurt. The fire that startled the sleeping inmates
of the rectory found an easy prey in the aged
walls and thatched roof. As the parents, who had
themselves barely achieved safety, counted their

treasures, one was found absent. The crumbling steps refused a support to the agonized father as he in vain attempted to ascend to the upper chamber where this apparently doomed lamb of his little flock lay still asleep. Returning in despair, he knelt and committed his child's spirit to the care of Him who gave it. Suddenly at the window the little one appeared. Two stalwart peasants—one climbing upon the shoulders of the other—placed themselves beneath, and as the crashing roof buried the spot where a moment before he had stood in jeopardy, they handed him in safety to his parents. Again upon his knees the father fell, calling upon his neighbors to kneel with him, exclaiming: "Let us give thanks unto God; he has given me all my eight children; let the house go—I am rich enough!" That the mother also recognized the hand of God in his preservation is shown by an entry in her diary. Alluding to one of her seasons of weekly retirement and prayer with him, she writes: "I do intend to be more particularly careful of the soul of this child that thou hast so mercifully provided for than ever I have been, that I may do my endeavor to instill into his mind the principles of true religion and virtue. Lord, give me grace to do it sincerely and prudently, and bless my attempt with good success."

Until the age of ten and a half years, this son remained under the tutelage of his mother; then, even at that tender age, was admitted a pupil at the Charterhouse, London. While congratulating himself on this great privilege—gained for him through the kind friendship of the Duke of Buckingham—he was well aware that many hardships would be his. His poverty and the cruel system of fagging, so long a disgrace to the schools of England, forced him to "bear the yoke in his youth." But he also proved the truth of the assertion that it is "good for a man" to do so. Such discipline resulted in a cheerful fortitude, a brave patience, an energy of character, which, combined with his studious habits, commanded respect.

How general is the ignorance that obscures the history of the childhood of great men! We naturally seek, after their names have filled the "trump of fame," to learn the details and incidents of their early life, when disappointment becomes our portion because of the meagerness or utter lack of what we seek. In the life of John Wesley we find an illustration of this; and while we should like to trace his boyish steps year after year, we find but little to gratify our affectionate curiosity.

We leave him now, after witnessing his election to Christchurch, Oxford, in 1720, at the age of seventeen; and while in these "academic shades" he passes the greater portion of the next fifteen years, we turn to other scenes, forming the antecedents of lives whose hopes and fears, whose joys and sorrows, we will endeavor to portray.

⇥ CHAPTER II. ⇤

IN the county of Surrey, in the year 1720, there was an old ancestral mansion—a "stately home of England"—enthroned upon a gentle eminence, which commanded from its rear an extensive view of cultivated field and fallow ground. In front, a park with trees of mighty growth obstructed the prospect, at the same time combining, by its size and variety, the advantages of tasteful care and the wild and beauteous grace of nature.

This home, so well calculated to be the abode of peace and happiness, had suffered a sad eclipse when, sixteen years before, the ruling spirit, the central figure, the domestic queen of this fair domain had exchanged her earthly home for one beyond the skies. Her husband, Sir Edward Dudley, who at the time was with the forces of Marlborough on the Continent, and whose last letter had been exultant with accounts of the victory of Blenheim, returned home with his General in December to find that his beloved wife had died three weeks before, leaving an only daughter to his tender care. His sons George and William were promising boys of eight and six years. His pride and ambition—and both were unbounded traits in his character—would doubtless be fully gratified in their careers; but when he looked upon his infant legacy, his heart melted in tenderness, and love outshone every

2

other feeling. In the delicate features, clear blue
eyes, and golden ringlets, he saw a miniature Ethel
once more before him. The likeness, most striking
as an infant, increased as the soul pervading the
beauteous casket shone out and informed her gentle
countenance with its purity and brightness. A
ray of merriest sunshine she was to the vacant halls
and echoing corridors. Never satisfied with the
comparatively small portion of the house in use,
she would make tours of discovery, and her nurse
would grow weary of following her curious footsteps wherever a willful fancy led them. Before
she could express her wish in words, she would
clearly signify her desire to be taken to the picture-
gallery, its attractions growing stronger year by
year, till at last, old enough to dispense with a
nurse, and her indulgent governess consenting to
her marked preference, it grew to be an understood
thing that Eva's play-room, study, and place of
general resort was the long room, isolated though
it was from her usual suite of apartments. There
would she spend hours surrounded by the ancestors
of by-gone ages—knights and soldiers, cavaliers
and priests, haughty dames and blushing damsels.
From the iron-clad Norman, grim and stern, to the
dashing courtier, with plumed hat, love-locks, and
laces; from the solemn priest, with gown and stole
and bands, to the lady of fashion, bedecked in jewels and costly array, or the innocent young maiden

in simple garb of white; from portrait to portrait would the admiring Eva go, studying lights and shades with the eye of an artist; marking expressions and features with the scrutiny of a pupil of Lavater; conning the dresses and armor, the weapons and ancient designs, with the discrimination of an antiquary and a lover of heraldry. It all resulted in a profound love for painting.

Her governess, who was prettily accomplished in the fashion of the day, could teach her embroidery or easy imitations of fruits or flowers; even sketches of the models that nature provided in murmuring brook or bending tree, in heath-clad hill or sloping vale, in ivied tower or grazing kine. But none of these satisfied the young artist; she yearned to depict on canvas the "human face divine," and innumerable were her efforts to produce satisfactory results. Complimented though she was by others, full well she knew she was but a tyro, and turning to her father, who had never refused her a request, she urged him to obtain for her a teacher sufficiently accomplished to gratify her desires. Sir Edward, who had little taste or appreciation for art, though his daughter possessed enthusiasm, was completely at a loss in what direction to turn to indulge her fancy. "Did she wish a master? she certainly should have one," was the purport of his determination; and not knowing what else to do, he forthwith wrote to his man of business in London, an hereditary lawyer he might be called, who, in his dusty chambers in Lincoln's Inn, knew as little about art as he did about the carol of birds, the rippling of waters, the softly springing grain, or any other of the sights and sounds of nature, to which he was almost a total stranger; and he cared less for it than for these.

While Eva was impatiently awaiting his tardy reply, her brothers returned home on a visit— George from Oxford and William from Eton. They soon became acquainted with the subject that chiefly occupied her thoughts. William encouraged her to go to London to take lessons, telling her she could persuade her father to agree to any thing she wished. Eva was reluctant to do this, however. She knew her father detested the city, and for her it had no attractions worth purchasing at the price of his sacrifice of taste and inclinations.

Too young for society, although on the verge of womanhood, her father regarded her but as a child, and indeed her pursuits and enjoyments were juvenile in their simplicity. Having been deprived of young companions, her brothers for so many years having been away at school, she missed the love and companionship of a mother. Her father, though thoroughly devoted to her, was undemonstrative to a remarkable degree. Her governess loved her tenderly, and Eva enjoyed her society and loved her in return; but she yearned for something more, and in place of that which she so much missed she made pets of birds and lambs, kittens and fawns, and nursed her flowers with a devotion rare to behold. So the thought of leaving all these dear dumb objects of her affection acted as a counter-balance to the attractive sights and sounds of even the great city of London.

George, differing with his brother, was in favor of his sister remaining at home. He was able to recommend to her, he said, an artist of high merit, a young man he had known at Oxford, who was so gifted that his friends predicted for him a brilliant career and wide-spread fame. He was poor, the son of a clergyman in Devonshire; had with great persistence and much privation gained his education. He had just graduated, and was now desirous of obtaining a situation as tutor in a private family. His ultimate plan and highest hope were to be a successful portrait-painter, "but," added George, "he is too poor to go to London and wait for patronage; he must first make money enough to support him there while he is establishing a reputation. Now," continued George, "I am quite sure if his salary as painting-master in particular to your little ladyship is as much as he could obtain as tutor in some gentleman's family, he would prefer devoting himself to the profession which he so passionately loves. I will speak to father on the subject, and if, as I suspect, he would rather remain here than go to London, I think there will be no difficulty in gaining his consent for me to write to Henry Woodville, offering him the position."

With many thanks Eva expressed her delight. Sir Edward willingly agreed to the arrangement, and in course of time the young artist became domiciled in the old manor-house. Had Eva's mother been alive, her keen maternal instincts might have taken alarm at this proposed plan, by which her young daughter, just budding into womanhood, ardent, affectionate, and romantic, was to be thrown into constant daily intercourse with a youth not many years her senior; and if she had not forbidden it, her watchful care would have hovered over them and sought to prevent too great a development of sympathy and regard. But Sir Edward viewed his little Eva as merely a child; her brothers did also. They had no idea of the risk they were running; no thought of the new element they were about to introduce into her young life which might so seriously affect it.

And so young Woodville came, buoyant with ambition and hope for the future; happy in his self-reliance and devotion to his art; handsome, impassioned, and intellectual, with a strong vitality and cheerful disposition that were at once a passport to the kindly feeling of all who were thrown in contact with him. In a short while he had captured the inmates of the old mansion. Sir Edward liked him because of his warm adherence to the house of Stuart, for the Dudleys were thorough Jacobites, and stout Sir Edward made but little secret of his partiality to the Pretender. George had been Woodville's friend at Oxford, so the congeniality that had drawn them together there continued and increased, favored by the auspicious surroundings of the leisure and retirement of the country. William could hardly understand how one so fond of manly, athletic, rural sports in which the young painter excelled, and for which he sought his company and yielded him his admiration, could at the same time be so literary in his tastes and so devoted to a pursuit that in order to win success would necessarily confine him to a quiet studio in the dusty town. To Eva—when the natural shyness of a little maiden, unaccustomed to other society than that of her own family, had abated—he seemed a creature from another sphere, and all the heroes of old romances and the embodiments of the brightest dreams of her girlish fancy sprung at once into life.

Henry Woodville was the only son of a mother in whose character firmness and discretion were so blended with gentleness and love that he had escaped the ordinary fate of only sons, and had not only been unspoiled, but developed into all that his mother's yearning solicitude could desire. Toward that beloved mother and his only sister he showed the

deference of a courtier, and so genuine was his
thoughtful politeness, so spontaneous and hearty,
that it had become interwoven in his being, and
by the gentle courtesy which in consequence marked
his intercourse with all females won from them at
once the most favorable regard. Eva's governess,
Miss Gilbert, was from their first interview his
warm friend. She recognized in him a likeness to
a dearly loved brother, who many years before had
been laid to rest in the quiet church-yard. Often
when Henry's ringing laugh would echo from the
court-yard below, or as from her latticed window
she would watch him with the other gentlemen
mount their impatient horses before taking one of
their frequent chases over field and fen, the tears
would unbidden come to her patient eyes, and backward the years would roll and she would see again
the distant, deserted home with all its familiar, beloved features, and the clustering curls and merry
eyes of the brother whom she had hoped would be
her companion through life, and support and solace
toward its close.

If such were the impressions made upon the various inmates of the Dudley manor by the new-
comer, it is not difficult to fancy how Eva regarded
him as their acquaintance rapidly ripened, and as
hour after hour of the long summer days were passed
in his society. Child though she was considered by
those around, and extremely juvenile in both ap-

pearance and manner as she truly was, her heart and mind were much more developed than her family imagined. Miss Gilbert's careful nurture, while she had imparted many graceful accomplishments and taught her the rudiments of much useful knowledge, had not stimulated her powers to their utmost.

The long conversations uninterrupted and absorbing, while Eva's hand was busy with pencil and brush, and her interested teacher hung over her easel, awoke within them both new resolves. The pupil discovered a craving for higher literary culture, while the young Oxonian determined to whet her appetite for the feast and then to indulge it by all the means in his power.

So much for the quickened mind. For the heart? —ah! no new resolves or determinations hastened *its* pulses. Slowly and unconsciously to each as time passed on, the current of their love—set in motion without their knowledge or volition by that magic, mysterious power implanted within our nature by Him who made us—flowed on, growing deeper and stronger with the passing months. How could it be otherwise? As young Woodville had come there expressly to teach Eva painting, and as she was enthusiastic in her desire to learn rapidly, her tasks with Miss Gilbert were abbreviated or neglected, and by far the greater portion of her time was spent in the long picture-gallery she had loved to frequent all her life. There, surrounded by the "counterfeit presentments" with which she was so familiar, and in imitating which her earliest attempts had been made, the days would glide rapidly away, while Henry Woodville would direct and suggest her task with eager interest and watchful care. As opportunity allowed he would read to her as she worked. At one time, leading her into the fields of classic lore, Pope's new translation of Homer's glorious poems would thrill her with military ardor, or "Plutarch's Lives" absorb her attention. Again, in the quaint pages of the "Faëry Queen" she would follow with delight the adventures of the "fair Una" and the "Red-cross Knight;" or the "infinite variety" of Shakespeare would move her mirth or pity, as comedy or tragedy occupied her thoughts. Sometimes the absorbing pages of De Foe would beguile the hour, and with "Robinson Crusoe" they would wander over the solitary island, or shudder at the inhuman feasts of the cannibal savages. Again, their companion would be Sir Roger de Coverley, and the graceful pen of Addison would elevate their taste, whether they lingered over the charming pages of the *Spectator*, or the classic lines of "Cato," or in his grateful hymn of praise, "When all thy mercies, O my God!" found an echo of thanksgiving awakened in their hearts.

Often on summer Sabbath evenings, returning from the village church, and Eva having recited her collects and lessons for the day to Miss Gilbert, Henry would seek her side; and under their favorite spreading hawthorn-tree, with the dreamy buzz of bees around them, and the gentle breeze lifting her golden curls, she would listen to his voice, which had now become perfect music to her ears, as he repeated the beautiful new hymns of Isaac Watts, or read selections from Jeremy Taylor's writings or Milton's majestic lines. She, however, enjoyed nothing more than the pages of that wonderful creation—that volume almost inspired, which is as fresh now to each succeeding generation as when first it was woven from the sanctified heart and brain of the humble John Bunyan—"Pilgrim's Progress;" a book which closely follows the Bible in every freshly obtained outpost of territory won to gospel light and literature; a book which has helped many a lowly Christian to bear aright the trials of life and meet death fearlessly. These Sabbath evenings were never forgotten by Eva through all her earthly pilgrimage. Though in after years her footsteps faltered on the rough pathways, though many a "Hill Difficulty" she had to climb, yet in retrospect this period of her life was always to her the "Land of Beulah" it then was, where the birds sung, and the sun shone, and the perfume of flowers filled the air. Truly the lessons of this book, which has been signally blessed of God, sunk into her heart, influencing her whole future life. Henry

had made her a present of this copy, and at once it
became the companion of her mother's Bible, which
Eva prized beyond expression.

So it came to pass that these two young people—
most congenial in tastes and character, and thrown
in constant intercourse—first knew of the danger
they were in when it was too late to recall the past;
first knew of the existence of their hearts by their
loss; and Eva awoke from her childhood by one
stroke, as it were, a loving and beloved woman.
To Henry, first, the revelation came; and, like
many another youth before him, he thought he could
stifle his feelings, crush out the affections of his heart,
by a strong action of his will, and at the same time
enjoy the dear companionship of the girl he loved.
For some months he deceived himself in this way;
and but for an accident which occurred about a
year after he had first come to Dudley Manor, he
might still longer have been lulled by a false security.   Possessing the keenest sense of honor, he
would have deemed it treachery to Sir Edward to
win Eva's love intentionally; so as soon as he became conscious of his own feelings, he resolved that
he alone should be the sufferer, and, by establishing
a stern guardianship over them, that he would give
no sign by word or look of the inward conflict; that
he would manfully and faithfully fulfill the contract
upon which he had entered, and for six more months
remember he was but the paid employé in the house-

hold of this rich man. Their kindness and familiarity he mentally declared should not be abused by him, for he knew the towering pride of Sir Edward, and that he would never consent for the only daughter of his house, in whose veins flowed blood transmitted through a long line of lordly ancestors, to wed with him, the son of a humble clergyman, without rank or fame or wealth. When his "term of service" was out, he bitterly thought, he would leave, and never look upon her sweet face again. She, all unconscious of his feelings, would soon forget him, the humble artist. Perchance in future years, when he had achieved distinction, his name upon the roll of fame, and pictures painted by his hand prized as choicest gems in collections of beauty and of art, she, in her high estate as wife and mistress of some knighted squire and lordly domain, would recollect when, long years before, in her girlhood, he had imparted to her knowledge and skill in his beautiful art, and, never dreaming of how he had loved her, would rejoice in his success and remember him most kindly.

Such was the programme Henry had marked out, such the vision the future presented. But ah! little did he know how weaker than green withes or new ropes would his resolutions prove, when the strong Samson of his love arose and burst them asunder like tow touched by fire or like threads; nor how all his strong hedges of defense would be swept away in an instant by the cyclone of passion aroused by sudden alarm for the safety of his beloved.

One afternoon Henry was wandering alone in the farthest extreme of the spacious park, and though dwelling upon his unfortunate love, his sense of duty in concealing his feelings and his resolves to finally and forever crush and bury them in his own breast were never stronger. He walked on, feeling the calm self-respect which is born of an acquitting conscience, though the heart may be sad and heavy-laden. Suddenly the clatter of horses' hoofs was heard approaching with fearful speed. Wheeling at the sound, he was horror-stricken to see that it was Eva's snow-white palfrey that was dashing toward him. Pale, erect, with teeth hard set and dilated eyes, she sat, her blue habit and long, fair curls streaming behind her. Her grasp on her reins was firm, but just as if by the lightning's flash the fearful scene was revealed to him, and as simultaneously he was revolving in his mind his best mode of action, the frightened animal swerved aside, and in a second Eva lay motionless upon the ground. To leap to her side, to perceive that she was insensible, yet not apparently bruised or bleeding, was the work of an instant. To chafe her hands, to move her into an easier position, was all that the poor fellow at that moment could do—calling upon her at the same time with every tenderness of tone and language, pouring out his love for her in the most impassioned manner, beseeching her to awake and live. Presently the faint color came to cheek and lips, the eyelids quivered and finally opened, and consciousness returned. *Returned!* Ah! It was a *new* consciousness that then came into being, for as the quickened ears took in the purport of the excited speech—as the fast-beating heart understood but too quickly and too well—the answering crimson dyed cheeks and brow; and in that moment Eva Dudley ceased to be a child, and experienced the bliss of "Love's young dream." With mingled ecstasy and misery, Henry ceased his ejaculations, and busied himself in brushing the soil and dust from her garments. Ecstasy—because in her whole face and manner he read the secret that he hoped yet feared to learn. Misery—because in spite of this secret, still more because of it, he saw at once that the time had come when he must leave this spot, which sheltered the dearest object to him on earth. With words of humble confession he then implored her pardon, telling her the whole sad story of his struggles and resolves, and how they had become worse than useless in this supreme moment of trial—adding that he would go away at once, and not disturb the serene current of her life; for hope could not enter his heart, knowing, as he did so well, her father's pride and ambition. But this favorite darling of fortune, who had never had a wish ungratified for one day in her life, could not think that now, when her whole happiness was at stake, her desires should be thwarted. With timid hesitation, yet with frank and ingenuous modesty, she declared her belief in winning her father's consent to what would be so vital to her. Was it any wonder that her confidence should inspire her lover with temporary hope? and as they walked to the house—for, fortunately, she was but slightly bruised by her fall, and the nervous trepidation of her fright had subsided before the consideration of weightier matters—he expressed his determination to seek an early opportunity for an interview with her father, and let her know the result as soon as possible. When, however, in response to his request, Sir Edward received him in his private office, and his brow grew darker and his lips more compressed and stern as Henry advanced in his story, the heart of the latter sunk, and he felt his former forebodings were more just than his recent expectations. The young man endeavored to do himself justice in the eyes of his senior, telling how he had been shocked into a confession of what he had determined to conceal. Admitting his want of wealth and high birth, but protesting that no blot was upon his lineage, and that with time and labor he could achieve fame and riches. With cold and haughty words did Eva's father assure him that life was not long enough for him to win the wealth and position necessary for a suitor to his daughter's hand. "It is not what the future may do for you, young man, but what the past has failed to do, that molds my decision. A Dudley cannot marry beneath her rank. '*Noblesse oblige.*'"

Eva's wonder was unbounded when, for the first time in her life, her father unequivocally and hopelessly denied her wishes. It must be owned that so far from viewing this fact as he did—that *because* it was the first time, her obedience should be most yielding and unconditional—she considered his decision the more unreasonable and tyrannical.

Of course the hours were few for Henry beneath the roof of Dudley Manor after his interview with Sir Edward. George and William were at their different universities; therefore, expressions of their opinions were not had upon the subject. A few short remarks from Sir Edward to Miss Gilbert signified that he considered her not blameless in this final catastrophe. So, divided between genuine regard for the offending youth and deprecation of her patron's displeasure, her words of farewell and of regret gave forth a somewhat "uncertain sound." Poor Eva in one brief interview declared to her lover that he should be her first, last, and only love. Exhorting him to disbelieve any possible future report to the contrary, she promised to wait indefinitely till he could come for her, and in the humblest cot with him she would be happier than enthroned as a queen.

3

Sir Edward Dudley, never dreaming but that the trouble was forever at an end, went to his pillow the night after Henry Woodville had turned his back on Dudley Manor and fell into a profound sleep, where he was visited by dreams of ducal coronets and heraldic emblazonments, court pageants and stately palaces, and Eva's fair young face was the central figure in each tableau.

→CHAPTER III.←

Two years rolled by. Eva had never left Dudley Manor. Her father had occasionally spoken of having her introduced at court, but she shrunk from the idea, protesting that she would be more content at home.

The first year she had heard nothing of Henry Woodville, but the second an occasional notice in a "news letter" of the day alluded to him as having painted a portrait of my Lady This or my Lord That; and poor little Eva, with her vague ideas of values and what constituted wealth, was encouraged to hope he was on the high road to fortune.

At the close of the second year, her father had business that peremptorily demanded his presence in London. So Miss Gilbert and Eva were directed to prepare for a journey to that city. They had been there but a few days when, strolling one afternoon in Hyde Park, Eva saw a well-remembered figure, and was instantly recognized by her lover. A short conversation assured each that their feelings were unchanged. Henry told her that he had been successful beyond his greatest expectations; and "if you were only a humble maiden," said he, "I could offer you a home of comfort and of ease."

"Dear Henry!" exclaimed Eva, "I am a humble maiden. My tastes are simple, my wants are few. I would not hesitate one moment to link my life with yours because of your lack of wealth —but how can I grieve my father? It is true your name has not been mentioned by me since we parted. Perhaps if he knew—I—I—loved you still, he might relent."

Their interview was protracted. It was accidental; therefore, the blame that would attend a clandestine meeting could not be theirs. But ere they parted their vows were renewed, and Eva had promised to speak to her father once more, and endeavor to remove his objections. Accordingly, with beating heart, she did so, only to find he was inexorable. No fault could be attached to the individual young man; the accident of birth was the insuperable objection—one that no personal merit could remove. In vain Eva painted his noble qualities, in vain represented that his family, while not noble, were meritorious and of good repute, refined and even cultured; the hereditary and traditional prejudices of her father were too deeply rooted to be moved.

While avoiding the least approach to deception, and declining interviews with young Woodville without her father's knowledge, Eva returned to the attack whenever a new line of argument presented itself to her; and finally her father closed a long debate with these words: " Eva, I am weary of the subject. I will *never* give my sanction to the marriage. If your special pleading could win my consent as your father, the duty I owe my king, my peers, my country, forbids the indulgence of any personal weakness of the sort. Once break down the barriers of rank, and the palladium of England's glory and renown is destroyed. Under this conviction, what matter the tears and prayers of a foolish girl? Still, your happiness is dearer to me than my own. If it will establish it to leave the father and brothers of your own blood, do so; I will not give you a father's blessing, neither shall alight upon you a father's curse. Make your election; but be assured the day you marry Henry Woodville you cease to be a child of mine." And in silence he left the room.

For several days Eva was in a state of indecision. Could her father really mean what he said? To have his curse withheld was a great point gained. Doubtless after awhile his blessing would be granted. If he could view the subject in prospect so calmly and dispassionately, surely when she was married he would relent and let her be his child again. "No child of his!" Eva almost smiled at the thought. Her father did not realize what he was saying. How could he banish her from his heart? No! no! He considered it his duty to speak thus beforehand, hoping to deter her from taking the irrevocable step; but if it was taken—she persuaded herself to believe—he would forgive, and receive her as his daughter once again. She little knew the calm determination of her father's character, or the strong hold the aristocratic principle to which he had referred had upon him, interwoven from his birth with every idea and thought of hereditary prestige and obligation.

Her brothers were absent, so Eva was deprived of their counsel; and in the full conviction that her father's displeasure would be but transient, in her youthful buoyancy and confiding love she showed most plainly to her not overprudent lover how little she anticipated permanent alienation from her parent. Woodville silenced his conscience to rest, persuading himself that Eva knew her father better than he did, and if she believed she would obtain a speedy reconciliation, his fears and scruples must be unnecessary. So easy is it to perceive reasons for persuading ourselves into a course of conduct we are anxious to pursue, that after Henry and

Eva had reached the above conclusion, the time
and place of their marriage was soon settled.   Immediately after the ceremony they turned their
faces to the home of his parents in Devonshire,
Eva leaving behind a hastily written letter to her
father craving his forgiveness.

In utter ignorance of their son's contemplated
marriage, the surprise of Mr. and Mrs. Woodville
was very great, equaled only by their dismay and
regret at the injudicious and hasty step.   With
the cool conservatism of middle life they viewed
the matter from a dispassionate stand-point, and
immediately decided that the bridal pair had married in haste but to repent at leisure.   They could
not believe that a young girl reared in luxury and
wealth could be permanently content with a humble sphere.   For their son, just as fortune had begun to smile upon him, and as he was entering
what promised to be a brilliant career, to so ham-
per himself with additional cares and expenses
created in their minds most serious forebodings.
Moreover, they had little hope of Sir Edward's
yielding his pride of place; and the hasty reunion
to which Eva looked forward appeared to them
dim and faint in its remote possibility.   Still, it
was impossible to know Eva without according to
her the place in their affections which Henry so
much desired her to obtain.   In a little while she
was the darling of the household, and the wonder

ceased that her young husband had allowed prudence, wisdom, and self-sacrifice to be vanquished by the love-light in her sweet eyes and the exquisite charm of her gentle disposition.

Their visit was short. Henry was anxious to return to his studio. He felt now that more than ever should he battle with life, and win from it fame and wealth to lay at the feet of his beloved. He was impatient to renew the struggle, while Eva soon became restless in her ardent longing to see her father, and hear his few words of forgiveness. Brief she felt they would be, but complete and satisfactory. So entirely had she persuaded herself into believing what she wished, that she fancied, even now, he had become reconciled to the inevitable, and was impatiently awaiting her return.

Upon arriving in London, Eva's first desire was to wait upon her father. Her husband, of course, accompanied her, only to find that he had left the city and returned to Dudley Manor. No letter or message had been left for her, and with intense disappointment the young couple established themselves in lodgings, and life took on a soberer hue.

Henry worked diligently, orders came in rapidly —from early to late he plied his skillful brush. Eva's great delight was to watch his masterly touches, and also to aid him in some of the less important details of his work. Had she but married with her father's blessing, she would have been supremely happy in her busy life, though far removed from her former station and luxurious surroundings. But this one sad fact—her father's displeasure—cast a shadow over her brightest moments, and only constant employment chased it temporarily from her mind. She had hasted, immediately on her return to London, to write to him a second letter, breathing much deeper penitence and far more yearning love than the former, and then with longing expectation she counted the slowly passing time ere she could hope for a reply. At last it came, and with beating heart Eva opened the package, directed in her father's writing, only to find her own letter returned—unopened! Poor child! the shock was very great. Days passed before she rallied. One evening, after long and dejected musing, with gaze fastened upon the bed of glowing coals before her, she raised her eyes to meet those of her husband resting upon her with inexpressible love, full of sad and tender sympathy. With a revulsion of feeling which astonished her she smiled brightly, and extending her hand to him exclaimed, as if answering his unspoken thought: "I do not regret it, Henry; I know I never shall! Much as I love my honored father, and deeply as I deplore, too late, his displeasure, you are far dearer to me; and henceforth, more than ever, shall we be all in all to each other."

This sacred compact remained unbroken through

their long and eventful lives. For several years fortune smiled brightly upon them. Henry had so far prospered in money matters that he had been able to provide a comfortable home and every necessary of life for his beloved Eva.

For eight years their little nest had been secure from the alarms and excitements of the outer world, and four little fledgelings had come to share it with them. Happy as a cherished wife, happy in her mother-love, absorbed in the care and education of her little ones, Eva's home would have been an Eden but for the recollection of her one sole act of disobedience, which was still unforgiven. Regularly every Christmas-tide would she write to her relentless father, believing each time that if he would but read he could not resist her pathetic appeals for reconciliation, or fail to consent to see the cherubs she so longed to show him.

Her brothers had occasionally visited her, and it was a great joy to her that their love was still unabated. Friendly intercourse with her former governess, Miss Gilbert, was still maintained, although the latter lived in another part of the kingdom.

So the years had rolled away peacefully and prosperously, in health and happiness, until the ninth summer of their wedded life, when disease seemed to fasten upon their household as if in revenge for his long banishment from their midst. One child after another was stricken, and for months the parents with heavy hearts would turn from couch to couch, scarce knowing which little sufferer demanded their attention most. When, wan and feeble though they were, their vigorous young constitutions conquered, Eva's joy was of short duration, for now life and death seemed engaged in a hand-to-hand conflict for her husband. Weakness and fatigue were all forgotten, and "watching the stars out by his bed of pain," she prayed for his recovery almost literally "without ceasing." Her prayers were granted and his life was spared, but his convalescence was most tedious, and months elapsed before he could be called a well man.

When able to attend to business once more he found that other troubles awaited him. His long illness, and that of his children, had enforced an empty studio and unused brush, which involved a cessation of income. Large amounts were due him, however, for work he had done—portraits of rich men, upon whose pleasure or convenience he had waited already till his patience was sorely tested. In vain did he present his bills—the selfish butterflies of fashion acted as if they thought the honor of having perpetuated upon canvas their vapid countenances was sufficient recompense for all his time and labor. Angry and disappointed he returned home after a fruitless day of severe toil, stooping to solicit with urgent words—because his needs were great—the money for which in truth he worked, but of which, like a true lover of his art, he never thought when the ardor of creative genius rested on him. His home-coming brought added care to his already burdened heart. Here bills awaited him; bills for the necessaries of life—for food and fuel, medicine and the visits of the physicians, and the grand total was appalling. Day after day these bills were pressed—he could find no means to liquidate them but by mortgaging his house, which he did with sad forebodings. It seemed to him the first step in the downward path of adversity. Indeed, it proved so; for, strange to say, for the first time in many years he found himself without orders. Heretofore his only difficulty was in being able to serve his oft impatient patrons, his diligence and rapid work being frequently supplemented by his wife's assistance. During his long, unavoidable absence from his studio, another artist had become "the fashion," and Woodville was obliged to acknowledge, with much chagrin, that the fickle throng had forsaken him to follow the rising star. It was hard—his hand had not lost its cunning, his eye was as true, his taste as pure as ever, but the current of popular favor had set in another direction, and he could not stem the tide. More than ever did he need money, for if at the appointed time the mortgage was foreclosed, the sacrifice would be immense, and ruin would stare him in the face. He sought pupils, and once more was glad to impart his knowledge to any who desired it. At the same time he began a grand historical picture which he fondly hoped would win a place in the Royal Academy, and eventually reestablish him in popular favor. Alas! his fate was like that of many others—strive as he might, the meager amount received from his pupils barely sufficed for daily needs. The hour of fate rolled slowly toward him, and with unspeakable sorrow and humiliation he was forced to yield his cherished home to his pitiless creditor, and go forth with his little family into the wide world, seeking a temporary shelter where best he might.

With all the heroic devotion of a true wife, Eva cheered and solaced him in this great trial. Her words of hope and tender love revived him as nothing else could, and he struggled on, endeavoring still to provide his dear ones with shelter, food, and raiment. It was impossible not to work with spirit, and hope for better days, when her sweet smile and cheery words and ways came to him as a benediction every morning, and crowned him with encouragement every evening, lighting up their lodging-place with the true light of home—the warmth of loving hearts.

Henry might have weathered the storm and their domestic bark been moored again in the peaceful haven of prosperous comfort and security, but once more the hand of disease was laid upon the "breadwinner" of the little band, and while its grim presence caused greater and unwonted expenditures, it at the same time was a barrier, insurmountable and cruel, to obtaining the income so much needed. This attack, though painful and lingering, was not as severe as his previous one, but still so tedious that his business difficulties assumed a far darker and more threatening aspect. Now he had no property from which to realize even temporary relief, and in a few weeks Eva had to endure the anguish of an enforced separation from him; for, O shame on England and her laws, at that time! he—a free-born, honest Briton, a man of education, culture, and integrity—was haled by the common sheriff to prison, for no crime, no fault, only a misfortune which health, liberty, and time might have mended, but which under that mistaken, cruel code made life a burden and drowned hope in almost rayless despair.

With her husband in a debtor's prison, and four little children depending upon her for support, Eva had no time for idle indulgence of grief, but rose to the demands upon her fortitude and industry with a heroic determination that deserved success, and in some degree won it. She visited her husband's pupils, offered to supply his place, and was received with but few exceptions. She called into requisition the lighter accomplishments of her girlhood and formed classes in embroidery, in flower-

painting, and in sketching. She had kept in good
practice with her music, for she had been the sole
instructress of her daughter, and now she obtained
several pupils—so by these means she kept the " wolf
from the door;" still his distant growls were heard,
for in addition to supporting her little flock she
had to care for her unhappy husband—to provide
food and fuel to supply his needs, those articles
furnished by the authorities being of the most mean
and meager sort. Eva could not bring herself to
write to her father now. While in comfort and
happiness she, out of the abundance of her love
and respect, could humbly sue for pardon; but
now, in dire distress and need, the pride she
inherited from him and the long line of ancestors
of which he boasted, that had lain dormant and
unsuspected by her all her life, asserted itself. She
felt that she might starve, but she could not hu-
miliate her husband and herself by seeking pardon
under such circumstances. If her path was hard
and thorny, she would walk in it without a mur-
mur.

Woodville's misery may be imagined, but cannot
be described. When he thought over the past he
tortured himself by supposing the results that might
have followed different courses of action, but his
devoted wife besought him to banish regrets that
were so unavailing, and constantly declared that she
believed that brighter days were in store for them.

Her visits to him were necessarily few and brief during the week, but on Sundays, with their little ones arrayed in their best, with food prepared the previous day, they would greet him at an early hour. Together would they read the service of the day, and sing the chants and songs of worship, instruct their children in religious ways, and commit their cause and themselves into the care of their Heavenly Father; leaving him, as evening shades warned them to depart, soothed and comforted by their society and affection.

Thus Eva struggled on, sustained by conjugal and maternal love, yet far more by her abiding trust in God. While to all human ken her lonely conflict seemed to stretch into interminable lengths, and hope for the liberation of her husband seemed far and faint, she never despaired. In the morning she "committed her way unto the Lord," in the evening she "acknowledged him," and the promise was fulfilled to her—"he directed her paths."

Winter merged into spring. Through the stone walls of his gloomy abode Woodville heard the chirp of merry birds and felt the warmth of the sunshine; while pacing the hard pavement of his narrow limits, he pondered over what "might have been," and longed and pined for freedom.

Summer came but brought no change, till one day while sitting on a stone bench in the quadrangle of the prison, almost in the apathy of despair,

Henry was startled by the unexpected appearance of his wife—unexpected, for he knew her business engagements seldom allowed her to visit him at that hour. Her cheeks were flushed, her eyes sparkled, and her whole appearance betokened a degree of excitement he had not seen her manifest for many a weary month. Hastily greeting him and expressing a desire to see him in private, she barely waited for the closing of the door before, throwing herself in his arms, she exclaimed: "O my husband, God has heard my prayers! You are to be liberated directly, and I trust a happy life, a long life of joyous freedom is before us!"

Scarcely crediting the evidence of his senses, Henry, almost overcome with joyful surprise, conjured her to be more explicit; and controlling her excitement, she continued: "It is so new to me, dear Henry, that I have not yet recovered from the great shock of happiness—if I may so term it—that I have received. Not one hour ago I was hurriedly walking through Regent Street, little dreaming how soon my path would be crossed by one who would bring us joy, when a gentleman accosted me, saying: 'Pardon, madam, but surely I have the pleasure of addressing a daughter of Sir Edward Dudley, of Surrey?' I looked at him in astonishment, but when he mentioned his name—Oglethorpe, of Godalming—I recognized an old acquaintance indeed, a gentleman who, being a near neighbor of father's, had been constantly at our house in my girlish days, and who had always shown a kindly interest in me. I must confess, dear Henry, that the unexpected meeting with so old a friend, bringing with it such a rush of thought, scenes of the past and present, was too much for my composure, and I burst into tears. Gently leading me to a retired spot near by, with all the tender sympathy of his noble nature he delicately drew from me our present condition; and the barriers once thrown down, I poured the whole history of our misfortunes into his friendly ear. 'My dear child,' he said, affectionately taking my hand as I concluded my recital, 'how rejoiced I am at this meeting! Be of good cheer! It is in my power, and most undoubtedly will be my great pleasure, to assist you materially. In fact, it is but for you and your husband to agree to my proposition and a new life is before you—a life in which the iniquity of imprisonment for debt is unknown, but assured liberty and probable competence, if not wealth, will crown the efforts of industry and economy.' Then, Henry, he proceeded to tell me at length his future plans, with which ours may be most intimately connected. He has been in Parliament for many years, and his attention and interest has been centered on—as he calls it—this blot on England's glory, the power of a creditor to deprive his unfortunate debtor of his liberty, and consequently the power to liquidate his

4

debt. He has succeeded in having a parliamentary committee appointed to look into the matter, and the result is that a number of prisoners have been released. Moreover, last month—on the ninth of June—he tells me, a charter was obtained from the king to form the province of Georgia out of a strip of land upon the coast not yet settled, and lying between the provinces of South Carolina and Florida. Liberal subscriptions are being received to assist the poor colonists, who are to be none others than—who do you think, Henry?—the unfortunate but honest, deserving debtors who have just been restored to liberty. How do you like the plan? and will you not be glad to share in its benefits?"

"My dear wife, you come as an embassadress from another world more bright and pure than this! How can you ask the question? At the thought it seems as if new life were quickening my pulses, throbbing in my brain, and animating these listless limbs. Methinks I can now breathe the fresh free air of the New World, and like the fabled bird of song, I am ready to rise from the ashes of a life of failure and disappointment to one of hard work, privation, and economy, yet of final and glorious success."

Eva gazed upon him as, standing erect, with determined air, he looked as if he would surely command the success he spoke of so hopefully; then, as his eye fell upon her, he added in a lower tone: "But you, dear wife, would you be willing to leave

the land of your birth and kindred to endure hardships of which you can form but little idea, surrounded by savages perhaps not always friendly?
Alas! I have already caused you too much sorrow,
too much privation; I fear I have been the bane of
your life; but for me you would now be in your
former sphere of luxury and of wealth."

"Hush, Henry!" interrupted Eva. "No wife
has ever been happier in her husband's love than I;
no mother more blessed in loving, dutiful children.
Our recent misfortunes were outside of that, and utterly beyond your control; they were our *misfortunes*,
remember, dear love, not *faults*. I have borne them
cheerfully, sustained by Him who has bid me 'cast
my care upon him, for he careth for me.' For my
one great act of disobedience to my father I do not
wish to excuse myself. Looking back upon it after
all these years have passed, I see now how I deceived
myself as to his views and feelings, but it was an
honest deception. I sincerely thought he threw the
onus of my misalliance—as he considered it—upon
me, and that when it was irrevocable he would condone the act. His rejection of me has saddened my
life, but I can blame no one but myself, certainly
not you. I was 'first in the transgression,' and
(lowering her voice) if he has not forgiven me I
know my Heavenly Father has. Therefore, dear
husband," she continued, "when my noble and generous friend comes to-day, as he has promised to do,

to set you free, I am ready with a thankful heart to
unite with you in any pledge you may make to him
for your future."

The benevolent and energetic Oglethorpe was
true to his word, and ere sunset had settled all of
Woodville's obligations, and had the great joy of
conducting him through the massive, gloomy portals of the prison and seeing him walk the streets of
London a free man.

In six weeks the little company of emigrants were
to set sail.   In the meantime Oglethorpe was pressed
with business, and perceiving Woodville's intelligence and activity, employed him as an assistant,
thus conferring two benefits upon him—the actual
wages he so much needed, also the glow of satisfaction and added self-respect at being employed in a
position of trust and honor, after the demoralizing
effect of a tedious languishment in prison.

Eva made the necessary preparations for their
long voyage and new home in another continent as
best their slender means would allow.   Her generous friend desired to add to her stores, and made liberal offers to that effect; but neither she nor her
husband would accept his bounty.   The liquidation
of his debts, which had caused his restoration to
freedom, was all they could be satisfied to accept—
for that they were profoundly grateful—for the rest,
they wished to fare as the other colonists.   Woodville felt his manhood stirred to its deepest depths

at the thought of wrestling with fate on virgin soil, beneath the sky of freedom.

Eva had written once more to her father, and fearing that it might be the last time she could ever do so, had poured out her soul to him in such melting words of love and tenderness that they would indeed have softened a heart of stone. Knowing the fate of former appeals, she had written on the outside these touching words: "Dear father, I implore you, *read*, for the sake of my mother's memory!" Alas! the postman was waylaid and robbed on Hounslow Heath, and the letter never reached its destination. With a yearning heart for her father's blessing Eva waited in vain, and at last left the shores of old England with the feeling of orphanhood stronger upon her than it had ever been. She had not been able to communicate with her brothers through all her troubles or before her departure, for William was with his regiment at Gibraltar, and George was traveling on the Continent, and their addresses were unknown to her.

At last the day for their embarkation arrived, and the little band—one hundred and twenty in number—set sail, with Oglethorpe as their commander and the Rev. Henry Herbert as their minister. The seasickness, which was a natural consequence of their life upon a foreign element, soon passed away, and Eva and her children were ready to enjoy with her husband the new experiences that

surrounded them. The long voyage was a fine pre-
parative to the life they would soon begin in the
colonies. They drew in great draughts of health
and strength with the invigorating sea-breeze.
Shunning the close cabin and staying on deck as
much as possible, each had the pleasure of looking
into the face of the other and seeing there the
healthful coloring, contour, and animation increasing week by week.

In Eva's baggage was to be found the Bible,
which was her daily study; the volume of "Pilgrim's Progress," dear in its associations with her
early love; and the text-books of her children.
Knowing that when they landed the days would be
crowded with busy employments, Eva used many
of the hours on shipboard to instruct her children.
It was a sight that won many a smile from their
leader as he glanced toward the modest little group
so engrossed with their occupation as to be quite
unconscious of his notice: the youthful mother so
anxious to "redeem the time" and train her little
ones aright, and the curly heads bowed over their
tasks, each intent upon pleasing that dear mother
and winning her loving praise. Then would she
gather them about her at sunset, and encouraging
their admiration of the glorious scene as banners of
gold and purple and scarlet would stream out from
the chariot of the descending "king of day," point
them to that land where the "city hath no need of

the sun to shine in it, for the glory of God doth lighten it;" or, while solemnized by the immense dome above them, at night studded by those innumerable worlds of mystery and light, she would lead their hearts up to nature's God through his wonderful works, and cause them to reflect on the power and goodness of their Creator, and the littleness and becoming humility of his creatures. "What is man that thou art mindful of him, and the son of man that thou visitest him?" Thus in every way this faithful mother tried to make the voyage one of profit and pleasure to her little ones, calling their attention to the wonders of the great deep, to the distant lightning's glare, or muttering thunder, and when the winds would rise and a tempest threaten, bid them fear not, for the God of the sunshine was the God of the storm, and when he saith "Peace, be still," to the restless waves, there would be a "great calm."

These children never forgot their mother's teachings during this memorable event in their lives. It was at this time they looked their first on death, and witnessed that impressive scene, a burial at sea. One little child had not responded to the healthful influence of old Ocean's breath. Delicate and drooping when brought on board, it continued to waste away till its little life was breathed back to God who gave it, and the tiny, waxen features, motionless in death, were for a few hours

longer granted to the tearful gaze of its parents.
Eva's sympathy was great for the bereaved mother.
Several times had she gone with her beloved ones
to the very portals of death, but they had all
been given back to her, and she had no little
grave to leave amid the mists and clouds of England. But now this poor mother must commit
this wee lamb to the ocean's depths, and never on
holy Sabbath evenings could she visit its resting-
place, and pluck therefrom one daisy to kiss and
weep over in absence and place beside the tiny
garments she so cherished.

The sea was like glass and the sky unflecked
with clouds as the little company, silent and un-
covered, stood to hear the words of the solemn
service. With awe the children gazed upon the
white object before them, so still, so rigid—the drapery "hinting and hiding" the dread secret beneath
it. Heavily weighted, at a signal it slowly slid
down, and softly disappeared in the watery waste, never to be seen again till that great day when the "sea
gives up the dead which are in it." With a shudder they watched the spreading circles around the
spot as the ship went on; and at night, as the long
column of moonlight shone above it, Eva used its
mild radiance as an illustration, like Jacob's lad-
der leading from this world to heaven—the angels
of comfort and of promise descending to the bruised
and wounded spirits here and helping them to as-

cend on the wings of faith and hope and prayer to that eternal home where all is bright, where tears are wiped away and there is no more sickness, parting, or death.

So the long voyage wore away, Woodville rendering himself of great service to his patron in many ways during its progress. We will pass over their arrival at Charleston, S. C., and the inland route to their new land of promise, merely stating that they arrived at the high bluff where Savannah is now situated early in the month of February, 1733.

Now, indeed, did their new life begin. With taste and wisdom, which the present beautiful "Forest City" plainly demonstrates, the benevolent Oglethorpe had the streets of the embryo town laid out with the greatest regularity. The houses, made of sawed timber, unplaned boards, and shingled roofs, were of one size and model.

Fifty acres of land to each freeholder! Henry Woodville felt that the future had great things in store for him when the deeds which constituted him a land-owner were put in his possession. He fancied himself at his three-score years and ten—having conquered the forest, and brought forth ample harvests year after year from the teeming fields—established in comfort under his own vine and fig-tree. Surrounded by his stalwart sons, educated in habits of industry and honest labor, the trials and mortifications of his early life in England would seem to him but a dream. Forgotten now was his former ambition as an artist. The only relics of that by-gone time were a small portrait of her mother that Eva had painted, enlarged from a miniature she wore that memorable day when she left her father's presence, never fancying it could be for such a long, long time; and a picture of Eva in her girlish days, care-free and heart-whole; with still another, holding her first-born in her arms. That little maiden was now ten years of age, and so closely resembled her mother that a portrait of her at that age was unnecessary, save that Ethel had seen too much of life, its disappointments, and its changes to possess the thoughtless and merry air Eva then wore. Her father called her his "little woman," and she was well named. She had been her mother's confidante and companion all her life, and it had sobered the joyous carelessness of childhood, and produced at times a pensiveness which added to her beauty. Two noble boys—Edward and Arthur—named for their respective grandfathers, and aged eight and six years, were anxious to go to work as soon as their feet touched the sandy soil, for "helping mother" had been their watch-word always; and the genius of labor, hand in hand with that of liberty, presided over the spirit of each colouist as he disembarked. Eva's youngest child—little Annie—four years of age, had been the pet of all on the ship, and many an hour had been beguiled of its tedium for the amiable Oglethorpe by her innocent prattle.

And now, leaving our colonists to carry out the plans formed for them by the trustees of the province—to clear the ground, to plant their flax and hemp and mulberry-trees—encouraged by the cordial welcome and treaty of the noble Indian chief, the truthful, faithful Tomo-Chichi, we will return to that Oxford student, whose path was soon to lead him to the same scenes, and whose work would be not to plant seed in the sandy lands of Yamacraw and Thunderbolt, but in the stony soil of human hearts; and God who gives the increase will see and take charge of the labors of both.

⇥ CHAPTER IV. ⇤

MR. WESLEY's life at Oxford for fifteen years was uneventful, and so self-absorbed and monotonous that it presents a striking contrast to his after history. In 1725, at the age of twenty-two, he was ordained deacon, and his first sermon was preached soon after at South Leigh, a small village near by. In 1726 he delivered a sermon at Epworth, his father's parish, and was elected Greek lecturer and moderator of the classes. His duties were interrupted the following year because of his absence in Lincolnshire, at Epworth, and Wroote, whither he went to act as his father's curate, his impaired health causing him to need an assistant. Here he remained almost entirely for two years. At the close of 1729 he was recalled to Oxford by the rector of Lincoln College, Dr. Morley, and there remained until he went on his Georgian mission in 1735. He was sent for to fulfill his functions as a fellow, and so became tutor in that college.

About this time an edict was issued by the vice-chancellor and others in authority to the effect that the college tutors should increase their efforts to teach their pupils the articles of religion and their Christian duty; to recommend to them the careful reading of the Scriptures and other books calculated to establish sound principles and orthodox faith. This edict, which was posted in most of the college halls, was called forth by the fear that infidelity, then so wide-spread, was diffusing its poison in their midst—a well-grounded fear, for the dean of Christchurch, being in sympathy with these pernicious views, forbade the posting of the edict in his college halls!

"The taint left by Charles the Second and his licentious court still festered in the higher classes of society," and down to the humblest rank in city and country the evil influence was felt. Here and there a few were found who had not "bowed the knee to Baal:" Gibson, Bishop of London, the Bishop of Winchester, and Butler, among those in the Establishment; among Dissenters, the saintly Doddridge and Isaac Watts; some devoted country curates who passed their quiet lives in a monotonous round of duty, unknown beyond the narrow limits of their humble parishes—"two or three berries in the top of the uppermost bough, four or five in the outmost fruitful branches thereof." But the clergy as a class were unworthy of their high calling, both in the ranks of High-churchism and Dissent. According to Bishop Burnet, who wrote in 1713, "the greater part of those who came to be ordained were ignorant of the plainest part of the Scriptures, and could give a very imperfect account of the contents of the Gospels, or of the Catechism itself."

It has been said of that time that "the Puritans were buried and the Methodists were not born." We know that "the disciples were called Christians first in Antioch." But, although Oxford Methodism began when Charles Wesley, William Morgan, and Robert Kirkham united for regularity in prayer and a weekly attendance on communion, during John Wesley's absence at Epworth, and was heartily joined by him upon his return, still it does not appear that the origin of the word was at that time. A pamphlet had been published in 1693, on its title-page alluding to the "New Methodists," and "their principles in the great point of justification." Still earlier — in 1639 — a sermon was preached and allusions made to "Anabaptists and

plain pack-staff Methodists.   Mr. Wesley says that
"the name was given in the time of the Roman
Emperor Nero, to a sect of physicians who taught
that almost all diseases might be cured by a spe-
cific *method* of diet and exercise."

Oxford Methodism! What was it? Mr. Wesley
wrote, "I considered religion as an entire inward
and outward conformity to our Master."   In pur-
suance of this idea, he and his band—the "Holy
Club," as they were called in ridicule—formulated
their lives.   Self-examination and prayer, self-
denial and faith, an endeavor to conform in all
things to the will of God, a humble avoidance of
spiritual pride, with a reaching after the full measure of Christian charity and earnest efforts to watch
over and assist in the spirituality of those around
them, were followed as the means of attaining the
inward conformity.   For the *outward*, blameless
lives of rigorous watchfulness, close study of the
Bible, making it their rule of conduct, stated and
frequent periods of private prayer, and meeting
every evening for union in prayer, reviewing what
each had done during the day just past, and consulting on plans of usefulness for the day to follow.
They practiced great charity toward the poor. Mr.
Wesley at first had thirty pounds a year; he tells
us that he lived on twenty-eight, and gave away
forty shillings.   The next year he received sixty
pounds, still lived on twenty-eight, and gave away

thirty two. The third year, receiving ninety pounds, he gave away sixty-two; and the fourth year, out of one hundred and twenty pounds he still lived as before on twenty-eight, and gave away the remainder. His executor states that in the course of fifty years Mr. Wesley gave away between twenty and thirty thousand pounds. He writes: "His accounts lie before me, and his expenses are noted with the greatest exactness. Every penny is recorded, and I am persuaded the supposed thirty thousand pounds might be increased several thousands more." In extreme old age Mr. Wesley writes: "For upward of eighty years I have kept my accounts exactly. I will not attempt it any longer, being satisfied with the continued conviction that I save all I can, and give all I can—that is, all I have." In reply to the commissioner of excise he once wrote: "I have two silver spoons at London, and two at Bristol. This is all the plate I have at present, and I shall not buy any more while so many around me want bread." So much for the practical illustration of love to his fellow-creatures.

He and his companions—for soon others, whose names are held in blessed memory, preëminently George Whitefield and James Hervey, united with them—endeavored in every way to do practical good to all within their reach. Some would visit the prisons, converse searchingly with the prisoners, read suitable religious books, and pray with them. They would contribute of their scanty means to buy books, medicines, and other necessaries for them, and when in their power paying the debts and liberating those who were confined on that score. Others would instruct and relieve impoverished families. Some would take charge of the parish work-house, and others a particular school, while all would endeavor to rescue young students from evil company, conversing with them, and encouraging them in a better mode of life.

Thus this little band lived, derided by many, but consistently determined to "promote the love of God, and the love of man for God's sake, to stem the torrent of vice and irreligion, and to fill the land with a godly and useful population." Twice in Mr. Wesley's absence their number dwindled away and almost ceased to unite, but revived and continued till first one and then another were called to other fields of labor.

Before his father's death, Mr. Wesley was urged by him and his brother Samuel to apply for the rectorship of Epworth, but it was inconsistent with his preference and views of duty at that time to do so. In justification of his desire to continue his work at Oxford, he wrote: "It is a more extensive benefit to sweeten the fountain than to do the same to particular streams." Finally, however, yielding to his brother's arguments, strong convictions, and advice as to what was duty, he yielded so as to indirectly seek the appointment, but failed to receive it, because of "disadvantageous things, misrepresenting the strictness of his life," having been spoken of· him before those who influenced the appointing power.

And now we have reached the time when the lives of the brothers Charles and John Wesley widen out, and they mingle in far other scenes than the peaceful shades of a literary retreat, and associate with far different companions than those whose chief end and aim was to be "most holy themselves, so that they could most promote holiness in others."

The Methodism begun at Oxford—"misty, austere, gloomy, and forbidding," though it might have been—was "intensely sincere, earnest, and self-denying." Far from perfect at that time, it had to struggle through many experiences, to undergo many modifications, before it reached the stature which it has since attained. For with Christian doctrine as with Christian character, not only individual souls but epochs and generations must "grow in grace, and in the *knowledge* of our Lord and Saviour Jesus Christ." For if with St. Paul, who "counted not himself to have apprehended," we pray that our "love may abound yet more and more in knowledge and in all judgment," "God shall reveal even this unto us," that with humble abasement we may cry: "O the depth

of the riches both of the wisdom and knowledge of
God! how unsearchable are his judgments, and
his ways past finding out! To whom be glory forever. Amen."

In April, 1735, Mr. Wesley's father died, and
soon after, while visiting a friend in London, he
met Dr. Burton, of Oxford, who was much interested in the colonization of Georgia. Dr. Burton
introduced him to Gen. Oglethorpe, who having
carried his first colony to the new settlement, had
returned on a short visit to England. He urged
Mr. Wesley to return with him on a mission there.
Upon consulting his mother, she replied: "Had I
twenty sons, I should rejoice if they were all so
employed!"

It is beautiful to contemplate Mrs. Wesley's character. How enduring and complete was the influence for good she exerted over her children! This
exalted reply was worthy of the deference and filial confidence that called it forth. No doubt it had
much to do with deciding his conclusion, for on
October 14, 1735, he embarked at Gravesend,
though a storm in the Downs, and a detention at
Cowes because of the man-of-war which was to be
their convoy, prevented them from fairly starting
till December 10.

General Oglethorpe returned to Georgia on the
same ship, and was courteous and kind to the entire party, consisting of the brothers Charles and

John Wesley and their friends Ingham and Delamotte. Here were three of the original Oxford
"Holy Club." Delamotte, a youth of twenty-one,
had joined them because of his personal attachment
to John Wesley. He served under him as a "son
in the gospel, did much and endured great hardship for the sake of Christ."

Again their *methodical* mode of life was renewed;
they formed rules to be guided by during the long
voyage, and every hour of the day from four A.M.
to nine P.M. was usefully or religiously employed.
They read the Bible and prayed together and apart.
They conversed or read with different passengers.
They catechised the children. They held public
service. They acquired languages or some science.
John Wesley studied German diligently, immediately prompted thereto in order to converse with
his German fellow-passengers, for thirty Moravians were on board, accompanied by their Bishop,
David Nitschmann, who had undergone severe persecution in the past, and whose godly conversation
was of much benefit and enjoyment to the ardent
missionaries, Mr. Wesley joining them every evening in their public service.

One incident related as occurring on this voyage
is interesting as showing the mildness with which
Mr. Wesley could rebuke whoever and whenever
he deemed it his duty, and the prompt candor with
which the great Oglethorpe could acknowledge an

error. The latter was greatly incensed because a
servant had drank up his private wine, the only
brand that agreed with him. "I am determined
to be revenged," said the Commander; "the rascal
shall be tied hand and foot and carried to the
man-of-war, for I never forgive!"

"Then," said Mr. Wesley, with great calmness,
"I hope, sir, you never sin."

Oglethorpe's anger was gone. He put his hand
in his pocket, drew out a bunch of keys and, throwing them at the offender, bid him take them and
behave better in future.

Another incident of quite a different nature is
well known. When a terrific storm burst forth
and threatened instant destruction, the English
passengers screamed in terror; while the Moravians, who were engaged in their usual evening service, continued calmly to sing their song of praise.
In response to his questions, when their prayers
were ended, they averred that they were not alarmed,
that even their "women and children were not
afraid to die." In an account of the storm, Wesley concludes by saying: "This was the most glorious day which I had ever seen."

How often our thoughts have dwelt on the dreams
that filled the brain of the "world-seeking Geno-
ese," as, with folded arms standing on the prow of
the vessel plowing for the first time the waters of
the "Haytian seas," he essayed to gaze into futu-

rity, and then recalled how far beyond his wildest fancy the glorious reality has been!

So also with Wesley. Other ordained ministers had preceded him to the New World, and constant intercourse had made it almost a familiar country; but *he* was coming as a missionary to the Indians. That was his chief desire and object; and we can fancy him as he paced the deck on star-lit nights gazing upon their countless numbers, and being thrilled with the remembrance of the assurance that "they that be wise shall shine as the brightness of the firmament, and they that turn many to righteousness as the stars forever and ever."

Then might his thoughts turn to the "untutored savages," and plans for their improvement and ardent desires for their Christianization swell within his devoted breast. Or, casting his eyes upon the ocean's broad expanse, he might look forward to that day, and long to assist its coming, when "the earth shall be filled with the knowledge of the glory of the Lord as the waters cover the sea."

But his broadest plans and most extended hopes for future success would appear to us meager and dwarfed in the light of the glorious reality. If, as that ship sailed on, with the veil of futurity closing before him, darker and more impenetrable than any clouds or mists that might befog her; if for one moment it could have lifted, and the great founder of Methodism, then all unconscious that he was to be such, could have seen the revelations of one hundred and fifty years in advance of that time, when millions of Methodists in Europe, Asia, and Africa, America, and the isles of the sea greet him as the instrument of their organization and the establisher, under God, of their faith, overwhelmed by a sense of his own unworthiness for so great an honor, we can picture him, as Moses of old, bowing before his Maker and exclaiming, " *Who am I*, that I should bring forth the children of Israel out of Egypt?" Or with Paul when he cried, "Who is sufficient for these things?" Then might the words of cheer and promise have flashed through his soul, "My grace is sufficient!" and with deeper humility born of the ecstatic vision, he would reply: "Not unto us, O Lord, not unto us, but unto thy name give glory," for "this is the Lord's doing; it is marvelous in our eyes."

But this revelation was not granted to him. No Patmos visions were his. Doing each day's duty as it came, seeking to know the one nearest to him, he landed at the new town of Savannah, consisting of forty houses and but a few hundred inhabitants. The court-house served also for a church, and the former rector having removed to Carolina, Mr. Wesley succeeded him by Oglethorpe's urgent request. This parish was not what he most wished; he yearned after the souls of the Indians; but, although Tomo-Chichi bid them welcome, and desired them to teach his children, promising to gather the great men of his nation, the time for their instruction was not yet ripe. As the friendly old chief was forced to admit, his people seemed determined not to hear "the great word" the white men had to teach, for they were in an excited state because of French and Spanish plots and treachery. Gen. Oglethorpe objected to the missionaries going among them, fearing entanglements that might result in injury to the young colony. Moreover, their rector having gone, the little parish of "Christchurch" was like sheep without a shepherd, and to take them under his care was plainly "the duty next to him." Convinced of this, he went resolutely to work, throwing his whole soul into labors unceasing—public prayers and preaching; teaching the children both religiously and in the rudiments of a common education; visiting from house to house; and acquiring the German, French, and Italian languages. He paid visits to the small village of Frederica and other settlements, being able, because of his recent studies, to hold service and expound the Scriptures to the French families at Highgate and Savannah and the Germans at Hampstead. Delamotte had charge of the day-school of near forty children; but disorder arose in it which he could not control, because the poorer children who were unable to wear shoes and stockings were ridiculed by those who did. Mr. Wesley, in order to peaceably adjust matters, quietly walked barefooted through the streets and into the school-room. His significant action had its effect—the poor were encouraged, the others ceased their jeers, and cast aside their shoes and stockings also.

The children loved him. To have his hand placed upon their heads in blessing was what they sought, often impeding his progress into church while thus affectionately attracting his attention; for he remembered our Saviour's injunction, "Feed my lambs," and did not merge it into that of "Feed my sheep." He established a Sunday-school in its best sense and most successful features—teaching the word of God with the view of bringing each child to Christ, and had the satisfaction of admitting some, at their earnest desire, to the sacrament of the Lord's Supper.

"Feed my lambs." A tender and imperative charge, coeval with that of "Go ye into all the world, and preach the gospel to every creature." And yet, for how many centuries was it disregarded, overlooked, neglected; the little ones not "suffered to come unto" Him who said, "Except ye be converted, and become as little children, ye shall not enter into the kingdom of heaven;" denied the "sincere milk of the word," the few crumbs that fell from the tables of the "sheep" unsuited for their needs and difficult for them to assimilate.

But at last this Christian doctrine and duty has become clearer. The generations have grown into this "grace and knowledge of our Lord;" "God has revealed even this unto us." Out of the long ignorance, carelessness, indifference, has come earnestness, energy, enthusiasm. Armies of little ones are marshaled, officered, by devoted and devout men and women. The most learned and talented of the Church deem it not beneath their gifts to prepare them literature; the sweetest songs of Zion are selected for their use; and surely the angels do not desire to look upon a lovelier scene than the myriads of children singing "hosannas to the Son of David."

More and more is the idea obtaining that to disciple the world we should "feed the lambs." In our country the conviction is felt that the future supplies to the Church must come from the Sunday-schools. In heathen lands the policy is adopted. Consecrated men and women are obeying the commands: "Go, and *teach*," "go, and *tell*." O how is it these little words have seemed so hidden all these ages? Have "our eyes been holden that they should not" see? How have we read this plain and obvious statement: "The angel said unto the women, Fear not, go quickly and tell. . And as they went to tell Jesus met them, saying, Be not afraid; go tell?" Thank God, we are reading it now with quickened consciences!

"Our eyes are opened, and we know him, and our hearts burn within us." "God has revealed even this unto us;" and now women, young, and tenderly cherished at home, are gladly leaving home and friends and native land, "counting it all joy" to go anywhere, everywhere—where God leads—to teach the children of heathen lands, to "bring them up in the nurture and admonition of the Lord," so that the future mothers and fathers in the next generation may be won to our Lord and his Christ, and the glorious day shall be hastened when their "sons may be as plants grown up in their youth, their daughters as corner-stones, polished after the similitude of a palace."

No doubt his intercourse with the lambs of his flock was unalloyed pleasure to Mr. Wesley. Other sources of spiritual enjoyment he found in the companionship of the colony of Salzburgers, who, having suffered severe persecution in Germany, had found a refuge in the Georgian province, some nineteen miles from Savannah, "and called the name of it Ebenezer, saying, Hitherto hath the Lord helped us." Their preachers—Bolzius and Gronau—were very much beloved by him; the friendship and testimony of the former particularly, through and after his painful experiences in Savannah, being of solace to him and value to his friends. The Moravians, with their Elder, Spangenberg, and Bishop Nitschmann—his fellow-voyager from England—

were also his dear companions and teachers. Having attained higher growth in grace and deeper experiences of God's dealing with human souls, they imparted to him their brighter knowledge, and by their means he was led to seek after the higher, happier life that they enjoyed. And so the two years of his sojourn in the New World passed away. He had occasion to "endure hardness as a good soldier of Jesus Christ." He had been in perils on the sea, and had waded through swamps, cold and hungry, to reach Frederica, where his ministrations were unwelcome after all. But worst of all, the trial of false brethren oppressed him. His life was a reproach to those who cared not to imitate him; and on the other hand, the extreme views of ecclesiastical discipline which he at that time entertained, gave serious offense to some who were brought within its bounds.

Before two years had quite expired, circumstances had so lessened his influence for good in his parish that it was the part of wisdom for him to return to England. It is useless here to narrate those circumstances. If touched upon at all they would necessarily demand such elaboration as would be inconsistent with the nature of these sketches. In Mr. Wesley's Lives exhaustive testimony is adduced to show that, while the rigid priest of the Church of England, imbued with the extreme High-church views which had marked him up to this time, he

might have had more zeal than knowledge, certainly
than love or patience, toward offenders; and while
the true spirit of his mind may have been endued
with the "harmlessness of the dove," it could not
claim the "wisdom of the serpent," still, the charges
against him were preferred by prejudice and prose-
cuted by malice. His final departure from Georgia
was such as to admit of severe comment by his enemies, but disinterested judgment sees in it only im-
patience of tyrannical and unjust authority over-
stepping its lawful boundaries. After exposure, fatigue, and hunger, he made his way from Savannah
to Port Royal, South Carolina, and set sail for England, December 22, 1737.

It might be supposed that having accomplished
so little where he had hoped for so much, Mr. Wesley would, in great discouragement of spirit, have
pronounced his mission to Georgia a complete failure; therefore the following extract from his works
possesses deep interest. He says: "Many reasons
I have to bless God for my having been carried to
America, contrary to all my preceding resolutions.
Hereby I trust he hath in some measure 'humbled
me, and proved me, and shown me what was in my
heart;' hereby I have been taught to 'beware of
men;' hereby God has given me to know many of
his servants—particularly those of the Church of
Herrnhut; hereby my passage is open to the writings
of holy men in the German, Spanish, and Italian

tongues; all in Georgia have heard the word of
God, and some have believed and begun to run
well; a few steps have been taken toward publishing
the glad tidings both to the African and American
heathen. Many children have learned how they
ought to serve God and to be useful to their neighbor."

In alluding in after years to the organizations he
had formed and the meetings for spiritual instruction he had instituted in Georgia, he says: "I cannot but observe that these were the first rudiments
of the Methodist societies; but who could then
have formed a conjecture whereto they would grow?"
Ah! who indeed? Doubtless Mr. Wesley himself
did not then conjecture, at the time he penned these
lines, even with the surprising experience he had
had, the gigantic proportions whereunto they would
grow, so that in a little over a century American
Methodism would number about four million com-
municants. It is evident Mr. Wesley did not consider his mission to Georgia a failure. Nor did
others. Mr. William Bacon Stevens wrote from
Georgia: "Was their labor here really a failure?
I answer, No! The failures of the Wesleys, and
especially of John, became as beacons to him in all
the future, and did more, perhaps, to shape his future than could possibly have been done by uninterrupted success and a perfect fulfillment of his
original designs." It is true that the testimony of

after years has been wholly to the effect that his sojourn there was productive of much good to himself and to others; but it is pleasant to know that
even at the very time when a combination of circumstances led him to appear more blameworthy
than at any other period of his life, such a prompt
and generous witness as the great George Whitefield,
who reached the colony only a few weeks after
he had left it, should declare that "the good Mr.
John Wesley has done in America is inexpressible.
His name is very precious among the people here,
and he has laid a foundation that I hope neither
men nor devils will ever be able to shake." And
he adds: "O that I may follow him as he hath followed Christ!"

Surely Mr. Wesley's history is an illustration of
the truth of God's promise to his faithful followers:
"In all thy ways acknowledge him, and he will direct thy paths." "If he had never come to Geor
gia he might have been known in history as a dis
tinguished presbyter of the Church of England; he
might have become a Bishop, or even Archbishop
of York, or Canterbury; but it is very doubtful
whether he would have become the world's great re
former." So writes Dr. Clarke in his "Wesley
Memorial Volume," and adds: "He has imperfect
ly read the history of Methodism who does not see
the special hand of God in conducting Wesley to
Georgia; the ship which bore him there in company

with the Moravians; the storm on the Atlantic which tried his faith; the intimacy with the Moravians Spangenberg and Nitschmann, and with the Salzburgers, Bolzius and Gronau; the trials, persecutions, vigils, fastings, and perils, in the solitudes of the wilderness, were necessary to form and develop the future revivalist and reformer for the great work to which God had called him. However viewed, they were as necessary to him as the residence in Midian was to Moses, the sojourn by the brook Cherith to Elijah, or the life among the captives by the river Chebar to Ezekiel. What Abel Stevens has written of Wesley's life on the deep, in the ship with the pious families of Herrnhut, may be affirmed of his whole life in Georgia: 'It was practical Methodism still struggling in its forming process.'" "*Its forming process.*" Let us mark the expression. How thoroughly in accord is it with God's works and ways, which physically and spiritually always inculcate the doctrine of "going on to perfection!" In the beginning God did create the heaven and the earth, but in his wisdom he made even that a work of time and progress. With Him who said, "Let light be, and light was," one word of power could have instantly spoken into being the green earth all habilitated for its human lord, with fowl and beast and creeping thing awaiting his commands; but he chose for unnumbered eons to let chaos reign. Then "the Spirit

of God moved upon the face of the waters," and by
degrees decided by his almighty wisdom, day by
day its own proportioned task was wrought, till
"God ended his work which he had made; and he
rested on the seventh day."

Even now how little do we know of this marvelous footstool of the Great King. "Oppositions of
science, falsely so called," are rapidly becoming
strong witnesses to his wondrous works, and will
soon unite in calling upon them all "to bless him,
praise him, and magnify him forever." Do we
summon the mammoth telescope to our aid and attempt to peer into limitless space? Bewildered and
weary with the flight, dazed by the wonderful revelations it discloses, our greatest conviction is that
we are but on the outskirts of an infinite series of
systems of worlds, and time is too short and humanity too feeble to grasp their mysteries. Do we turn
to the microscope and, congratulating ourselves
upon the vast information it has bestowed, seek to
exhaust its capacity for teaching us? Baffled again,
we can but abase ourselves before the Great Creator, and acknowledge that his ways are past finding
out. Do we attempt to fathom the "treasures of
the hills," or seek amid the "testimony of the
rocks" proof to satisfy us that God's work is complete and we can understand its use and meaning
fully? Far otherwise is their evidence—for con-
vincingly do we see that in that vast store-house of

"never-failing skill" in silence and darkness are being worked out results that demonstrate his great
power and kindness to the human race. Slowly
the vast areas of coal are formed; gradually are
accumulated those reservoirs of oil which now are
being poured out in rich and abundant streams for
the use of man. In our ignorance we cannot sur-
mise the blessings that may yet be given us out of
these hidden chambers where the Divine Architect,
by his slow and secret process, is working out his
vast designs. In the "fullness of time," as in his
wisdom he sees fit, God will reveal it to us. Or, if
it is true that in this sense "the thing that hath
been it is that which shall be, and that which is
done is that which shall be done, and there is no
new thing under the sun;" and if in some distant
world creatures of superior intelligence look down
upon our puny efforts and smile at what we call
our "great discoveries," and our "new and improved methods," and compare our "grand and
modern achievements" with far abler and nobler
works that were done ages ago; and even as time
rolls on, and as year after year some patient worker
in our day catches a glimpse of a lost art, a lost
language, a lost race, and vaguely speculates as to
what may yet be hidden, and wonders if more of
human knowledge and of skill has been erased by
the hand of Time than now triumphantly flaunts
its achievements in the face of day—what then?

6

Still it remains true that God's forming process is yet going on for the benefit of each succeeding generation; for if to man—the great crowning work of creation, made in God's image and likeness—has been given "dominion over all the earth;" if to him the angels are sent as ministering spirits, and it is declared that there is "joy in their presence over one sinner that repenteth," then surely for him the vast deposits within the bosom of this green earth are formed; and the hidden fires weld and forge; and its spacious, mysterious laboratory is at work; and the patient coral toils and rears its beauteous structure; and wind and wave, and all animate and inanimate forces, combine to serve and bless him.

Yes, *growth*—which expression is but a synonym for the forming process—is the law of God. As an eloquent writer* remarks: "We cannot exhaust the sources of study and research, even in this small part of the universe we call the earth. New fields open up daily; new forces, or old forces in new forms of development; new applications of known laws, and new possibilities, challenge the ambition of men, and no horizon to human progress presents itself in the distance." If this is true in physics, and to a great extent in metaphysics, must it not also be of our spiritual natures? Verily, yes! We are assured of it in God's revealed word and in our

* Dr. W. P. Harrison.

very consciousness. Such is the experience of every
thoughtful soul striving to rise higher, and whose
profound breathing is, "Nearer, my God, to thee."
Therefore we are not puzzled by all that has been
written about Mr. Wesley's spiritual condition when
he was in Savannah. We read of his dissatisfaction
with his experience at that time, and of the greater
knowledge of a "life hid with Christ in God" that
he obtained from his intercourse with the devout
Moravians and Saltzburgers, and we believe with a
recent author * "that the difference between Mr.
Wesley's spiritual life in Savannah and his subsequent life—for which the former prepared him
—was indeed great; but it was no greater than the
difference between Moses before and after his experience at the burning bush, between Isaiah before
and after his lips were touched by one of the seraphim with a live coal from the altar, or Peter before
and after Pentecost. It was no greater than the
difference between a babe in Christ, or a young man
who has overcome the wicked one, and a father in
Israel who has known Him that is from the beginning. And it was no greater than the difference
between St. John before and after he received the
perfect love which casteth out fear. Mr. Wesley's
self-condemnatory expressions at this period of his
life no more make against the soundness of this
opinion than the like condemnatory things which

* Dr. J. O. A. Clarke.

many Old and New Testament saints recorded against themselves prove them to have had, at the time they uttered them, no real experience in the things of God."

For the utterances of these saints we "thank God, and take courage," knowing assuredly that the book which records their sins and short-comings so faithfully, without apology or extenuation, is true, and if they have "washed their robes and made them white in the blood of the Lamb," and now rejoice in his presence forever, we can follow them— not in the errors that caused them tears of repentance, but as they followed Christ.

We may well believe that "the entrance of God's word, which giveth light, revealed to the spiritual sense, with every increase of light, imperfections it never saw before;" therefore Mr. Wesley, dissatisfied with his spiritual attainments, at one time feared he was not converted; therefore Job, a "perfect and an upright man, one that feared God and eschewed evil," when he saw more of God's power and goodness "abhorred himself, and repented in dust and ashes;" therefore St. Paul declared that he had not already attained, or was already perfect, but that he followed after and pressed toward the mark; therefore cherubim and seraphim veil their faces before Him in whose sight the heavens are not clean, and who only is absolutely and infinitely holy. Then, with this increase of light, of self-knowledge and self-abasement, comes the more rapid growth and the higher attainment. As in the natural so in the spiritual world—"first the blade, then the ear, then the full corn in the ear." As ascending some mountain peak the horizon widens the higher we go, ever revealing new and unsuspected distances and landscapes of surprising beauty, so as we near the summit of the mount of God experiences may be vouchsafed to us of which we never dreamed—Pisgah views, a foretaste of the heavenly Canaan. But only a foretaste; still, "More and more" can be our watch-word; for as long as we "see through a glass darkly," and "know but in part," so long can we but comfort ourselves with these words: "Eye hath not seen, nor ear heard, neither have entered into the heart of man, the things which God hath prepared for them that love him;" for then, and not before, "shall we be satisfied when we awake with his likeness."

→CHAPTER V.←

LETTER from Mrs. Eva Woodville, of the town of Savannah, in Georgia, to Mrs. Mary Gilbert, of Lincolnshire, England:

"FEBRUARY 2, 1738.

"*My dear and honored friend:* To-day is the anniversary of our landing on the shores of our new home, and I cannot celebrate it more pleasantly to myself than in writing to you the letter which has been so unwittingly delayed, and in doing so recount and review the mercies of the past five years. For truly, if my memory retraces the occurrences of all that time, from a full heart will I be prompted to exclaim, 'What shall I render unto the Lord for all his benefits?'

"From the letters I have sent you heretofore you know that since the day I met our beloved friend, Mr. Oglethorpe, in Regent Street, I have had cause to thank God that our paths then crossed; for the change that interview has caused in the lives of myself and family has been for good and good only since that hour.

"The voyage across the Atlantic was of incalculable benefit to us all. New life seemed to be infused into us—strength, vigor, a cheerfulness and an energy—which has never diminished. The relaxing climate of summer has had no evil effect upon us. We have avoided the meridian sun, and carefully shunned the dews of night; we have observed the strictest sanitary precautions, and our health has been unimpaired. The labor of our hands has been blessed. You have expressed apprehensions that my daily duties have been or would be too great for my strength. Ah, dear friend, strength has been given me for every need. I have learned, long since, to live day by day. Are we not taught to ask for our 'daily bread?' And surely our Heavenly

Father means not only the 'meat which perisheth,'
nor merely fresh supplies of the 'bread of life,' but
a sufficiency for every need of the body, the mind
and soul, which he has made; therefore I take but
one step at a time, and the rough places are made
smooth, and I go forward rejoicing. I do not believe there is a happier woman in this colony I
believe I would be perfectly happy if the cloud of
my father's displeasure were lifted from me. Often
in balmy evenings, my work all over for the day, I
sit beneath our porch of vines and picture his dear
face as I fancy it with the added lines of sixteen
years—for it is that length of time since I beheld it.
Ah well! one of these days he will know how I
longed and pined to see him and to tell him how
much I ever loved him—if not before, surely in
that good world where we may hope to meet at last;
and doubts will be cleared, and puzzles solved, and
explanations made, and wrongs righted, perchance.
I have always believed if he had but read my last
letter, written on the eve of my departure from
England, he would have relented.

"I said the labor of our hands has been blessed.
It is even so—yea, abundantly. Our wise leader's
first act was, as I have told you, to convene us all
the morning after we landed, and formally to thank
God for our safe arrival, and implore his future
blessing upon us. Then, after listening to his words
of kindly advice on many subjects, the busy hive

swarmed to the various important duties demanding
immediate attention.   Days and weeks passed away,
and homes were finally established, and the delightful sense of proprietorship animated many reviving
breasts that had once been filled with sorrow—
almost despair.   The giant forest-trees fell before
the stroke of the axman; the rich soil was easily
prepared for culture; no stones, ravines, or worn-
out spots to conquer or redeem, but a soft and level
sward rendered the task comparatively light; and
sooner than we deemed it could have been, we
proudly looked upon 'our crop,' greenly beautiful;
saw our mulberry-twigs budding in promise, and
the prospect of sitting under our own vine and fig-
tree coming nearer every day as the tender shoots
we watched grew larger.

"You cannot know, my dear friend, the joy and
pride I felt in watching my husband as with mus-
cles hard and tense he wielded his ax upon a towering primeval pine, turning to cast upon me a look
of triumph as, standing erect upon its prostrate
trunk, he wiped his glowing face—each of us knowing that the other regarded the act symbolical of
our life in this New World.

"Our children partake of this spirit, and their
willing, eager little hands and feet lighten our labor
by help you might be surprised to see them render.
Ethel, you know, is now fifteen years of age.   Her
outdoor life has developed her into a woman in ap-

pearance, taller than her mother, while the varied experiences of her life have caused her mind and heart to keep pace with her outer stature. Edward and Arthur are robust sons of the forest, I was about to say, for they not only assist their father in all his occupations, but have learned wood-craft and sports of various kinds from the young Indians of Yamacraw. The noble old chieftain, Tomo-Chichi, is a special friend of ours. Often he spends hours with us, and the legends of his forefathers which he relates to us enchains the attention of our entire circle. It is impossible to compute how much the colony is indebted to him. If so inclined he could have been the means of our irretrievable ruin. At his suggestion the neighboring tribes might not only have greatly annoyed us, but it was easily in their power to utterly destroy us. But we live unmolested near them, and without a fear of their unfriendliness. This generous chief's kindly attitude toward us, combined with our noble leader's discreet and wise addresses to their warriors, has established the latter's confidence in our good feelings toward them. The conciliatory policy of Mr. Oglethorpe has been eminently successful. The treaty which he made with the lower Creeks shortly after our arrival here has been preserved inviolate. They gave to us all lands lying between the Savannah and Altamaha rivers, from the sea to the head of tide-water, and all the islands along the coast

with the exception of three—Ossabaw, Sapelo, and
St. Catherine—which they reserved for hunting,
bathing, and fishing.   They agreed that they would
abide by the laws of England, and all criminal cases
should be tried thereby; admitting that the Great
Power which dwelt everywhere, and had made both
them and us, had given to the pale faces more wisdom, and had sent them hither for their instruction.
When we hear of the frightful cruelties that have
been suffered by the settlers of other colonies, and
of the relentless hate and vengeance of the Indians
toward them, our admiration and gratitude for the
prudence, judgment, and wisdom of Mr. Oglethorpe,
and the generosity and friendship of Tomo-Chichi,
must ever increase.

"Doubtless you wish to know how our towns are
prospering.   You have heard of the good Salzburgers at Ebenezer.   They became dissatisfied with
that site for various sufficient reasons, and obtained
permission to remove a few miles to another loca-
tion, that pleased them better, which they called
New Ebenezer.   They are a pious, industrious, and
quiet people.   By the aid of friends in Germany
they have been able to build two comfortable houses
of worship.   One in their town is called 'Jerusalem Church;' the other, four miles on the road to
Savannah, is named 'Zion Church.'   With their
two faithful and devoted pastors—Rev. Mr. Bolzius
and Rev. Israel Gronau—they hoped to have had

both pulpits filled and to have done much good, but alas! the latter's day of usefulness was nearly over for calling upon the Lord, whom he had served for so long, to 'come quickly.' He has lately entered into rest. The Salzburgers are accomplishing more in silk-culture than any settlement in the colony. Their patient painstaking obtains its reward. The Moravians are equally devout and industrious. Amid the lawlessness that sometimes rears its head and looks around for countenance, such conservative, law-abiding elements are of extreme value.

"The colony of Scots at New Inverness—or Darien as they now call it—are a hardy, brave, and determined set of men. They have a fort and four pieces of cannon. They dress in their Highland costume, with broadsword and target. We feel as if they are a defense for us between the Spaniards, who love us not, and our simple but beloved homes.

"The town of Augusta, on the Savannah River, has become a trading mart of consequence. Warehouses have been built to hold the goods suitable for the Indian trade. Great numbers of Indians come there at certain seasons, and it has more traffic with them than has any other town in either Georgia or South Carolina. A road has been opened from that point to Savannah capable of being traveled on horseback, and the future of the namesake of the Princess Augusta looks very bright.

"The settlement of Frederica, on St. Simon's

Island, to the south of us, has grown rapidly as a military post. Mr. Oglethorpe recently spent a pleasant hour with us, and we found his conversation about this new town both interesting and instructive. It is situated in the midst of about forty acres of cleared land—for it was an old Indian field. The bluff upon which it stands is ten feet above high-water mark. The fort is so situated as to command the river above and below it. The harbor is deep and protected by the land so as to afford safe anchorage for many large ships. In addition to these advantages, the beautiful forest-trees, the abundant game, and various kinds of fish make it a delightful home, provided the Spaniards are kept away. Mr. Oglethorpe does not fear them. The Indians are our friends, or the most of them are, and he has established a system of outposts and scouts upon whom he depends to inform him of their movements and disposition toward us. At all events, it is the best point for a military post; and if an attack is ever made by them, he is preparing to meet it.

"The houses there, he tells us, are built of tabby, a mixture of lime made of oyster shells with sand, small shells, etc., which when hardened becomes as firm as stone. This cement, when soft, is poured into molds, and so the walls are hardened entire. They present a picturesque appearance, handsomer than you would suppose, very durable, and calculated to resist the action of fire. But, although the site of this town is so beautiful, and it presents so many desirable conditions, I am glad our lot is cast in Savannah—upon the main-land, and not upon an island.

"I wish you could see the beautiful forest-trees in this favored country. The magnificent live-oaks, with their graceful drapery of gray moss forming natural arches and vistas such as no cathedral of human architecture can imitate, seem truly God's temples not made with hands. The splendid magnolia-tree we consider a wonder of beauty—tall and straight, its smooth bark, and its glossy leaves rich green on top and the lower side a silky brown. Its flowers, large, white, and velvety, with a delicious fragrance that fills the surrounding air, would make it the pride and pleasure of an English park. Our children love to gather the snowy petals, and with any sharp instrument—a pin or thorn—trace characters thereon, watching the changing colors as they write, for a dull brown follows each stroke of their pen, and every word is indelible. You, my dear friend, have often remarked my inclination for drawing lessons from all around me wherewith to instruct my children, so you will quickly see how natural it was for me to tell them that the pure white magnolia-leaf, with its ineradicable stains so easily made, reminded me of our souls; not that they are spotless naturally. Alas!

no.   But the stain of sin can be so quickly left upon them, and no effort of ours can ever erase the dark spot; only He can who has said, 'Though your sins be as scarlet, they shall be as white as snow.' Indeed, we are encouraged to ask Him to wash us, and we shall be 'whiter than snow.'

"But to return to the ornaments of our forests, of which I wish to tell you, for I know how dearly you love natural growth of every sort. The orange-tree perhaps is nearer perfection than any thing that grows. Symmetrical in shape, luxuriant in foliage, fragrant in leaf and blossom, with fruit as delicious as beautiful, imagination can suggest no added charm. As I write I view from my window one that might have been transplanted from Eden. As the sunshine glances on it, and the soft south wind bears its perfume to my delighted senses, the glossy green leaves shimmer and rustle, the snowy buds and blossoms exhale their choicest odors; the fruit in rich profusion, green and golden balls, perfects the picture. Were you by my side, quickly would I pluck some and let its excellences appeal to another and very appreciative sense. Pause over my description one moment, dear friend, and note the unusual fact that at the same time blossom and fruit, both ripe and immature, are to be found upon the tree. This is no uncommon thing—it is its natural habit. Time and space forbid my dwelling at large on the trees and shrubs of this sunny land. Delightful

fragrance is a distinguishing peculiarity of very many
of them—the cedar, the bay, the myrtle, the sweet-
gum, the sassafras, each is charming in its turn. Even
the towering pines, with the soft carpet beneath our
feet, formed by their fallen, needle-like leaves, possess a pungent, resinous odor which is most pleasant. And what shall I say of the vines? The
wild-grape blossom combines with the delicious jes-
samine to load the air with perfume. The latter,
wreathing the trees with gay garlands of yellow,
trumpet-shaped flowers, would invite you to trans-
fer its beauty to paper or canvas with as little delay as might be.

"My children have warmly seconded my efforts
to make our new home attractive as well as comfortable; and while my husband and boys are occupied with their labors in garden or farm, Ethel,
Annie, and I have succeeded in our efforts, and
vines and shrubs embower our home, and we think
it a lovely spot. We transplant from the forest
many beautiful things, and I have sown the seed
of flowers I brought with me from old England, so
now many familiar plants and blossoms smile at
me as I tend them.

"I think I told you our town-lot is sixty by
ninety feet; but near by we have a garden of five
acres, and farther off a farm of fifty. The sun is
warm in the middle of the day almost the entire
year; so we rise with the lark, and the warmest

hours we spend in-doors. My husband and sons have been very successful in their work, and all our needs are well supplied.

"There is a desire among some to obtain negro slaves, and a request to that effect has been proffered more than once to the trustees of the province, but they have not consented. Public opinion is much divided on that subject. They are in South Carolina in large numbers, but the Spaniards tamper with them, and many leave their owners, frequently to their great annoyance and expense. I confess I am not much interested in the subject. As we are too poor to buy any, the question does not affect us. Poverty here is very different from what it is in England. In Lincolnshire we would not think a peasant very poor with a comfortable house and fifty-five acres of fresh land, rent free. And truly, by contrast and in recollecting the past, I do not feel poor here. All our necessities are abundantly supplied; and since my sturdy boys have grown large enough to pursue the manly sports of hunting and fishing, my larder is never without the results of their skill. They have made associates in these employments with our red neighbors of Yamacraw, and two or three braves are most kind in taking them with them on such excursions. No protected park or well-stocked preserves forbid their entrance, but free as the air and the sunshine is water-course or forest; so all that they can yield—and the variety is immense—becomes in turn supplies for our table, healthful, delicious, and inexpensive.

"In the midday hours of rest, my husband teaches our home school. Being an Oxford graduate, as you know, and possessing an aptitude to teach, and our dear scholars desiring to learn, and certainly not dull, I confess I am more than satisfied with their progress.

"You asked me if Henry ever painted now. Only two pictures since our arrival here—one a portrait of our benefactor, dear Mr. Oglethorpe, in which he has caught his noble expression most admirably, and a no less happy likeness of the good Tomo-Chichi. These twin pictures, painted with details to correspond and render them such, we teach our children to value as the originals deserve. Our request is that they shall never be alienated, for I doubt not the time will come when our descendants will prize them, and dwell upon the histories and deeds of these great and good men when our individualities if not names are forgotten. Indeed, dear friend, as I gaze upon them and think of the long rows of family portraits in the picture-gallery at Dudley Manor, I can think of none for which I would exchange these, dear to my heart by ties of gratitude and personal affection. Of course I except my parents' and brothers' portraits. I possess duplicates of the former, painted, you recollect, after my marriage from miniatures I owned. The

7

latter I have reproduced from memory since I have been here, and Henry pronounces them good likenesses. I show them to my children, and endeavor to win their love for their unknown relations, but they do not evince the cordiality I would like to see. Too respectful to me to fully express their feelings, it is evident that resentment at the silence of their kindred toward me is the chief sentiment they experience. When I picture to them the England of my earlier years, the interest and admiration I desire to elicit in most of its institutions, its customs, and mode of life are overshadowed by the thought of the cruel injustice their father suffered because of an unrighteous law. Their respect and admiration for him are unbounded, and the remembrance of his incarceration in a debtor's prison and the painful details of insolence and unkindness he there endured arouses a degree of anger in them that I endeavor to obviate by discouraging all references to that sad past. They are very disloyal little colonists in other respects also, and declare they would not exchange their free life with its prospects here for all that the Old World could offer. Our boys' admiration for our noble Governor throws a halo around his whole enterprise, and they hesitate not to profess that they are his subjects, and not King George's! I must own that they show much discrimination for boys so young. When passing in review the heroes of antiquity, they declare none can compare with him in grand achievements or personal character.

"'Who was Alexander the Great,' exclaimed Edward, 'but a great robber on an immense scale, carrying terror before him and leaving desolation behind?'

"'And Julius Cæsar?' replied Arthur sententiously. He wished to subvert the liberties of Rome.'

"'William the Conqueror's victories were for his own pleasure and aggrandizement,' continued Edward.

"Arthur rejoined: 'And Romulus, if he was the founder of Rome, laid its foundations in blood, for he was the slayer of his twin brother.'

"'While Col. Oglethorpe'—for, as you know, he has recently received his commission from the king —'while Col. Oglethorpe,' said Edward, 'has voluntarily left a career in his native land which promised distinction and increase of wealth, and all the comforts and pleasures of home and friends, in order to extend the dominions of his king——"

"'And to promote trade, and civilize and Christianize the Indians, father says,' interrupted Arthur.

"'Surely, boys,' I interposed, 'we must not forget his humane thought for the relief of the poor and distressed he brought with him.'

"'What an example he has set us,' said my gentle Ethel, 'of self-denial and fortitude—sleeping upon the ground without shelter often, and his food as plain as the poorest soldier's.'

"'What does he care for that?' cried my sturdy Arthur, who affects an Indian's indifference to hardship and fatigue. 'I admire him because he is so just. He will keep his word to the humblest Indian, and he shall receive justice at his hands as surely as if he were a prince.'

"'Yes,' said Edward, 'Toonahowi (Tomo-Chichi's adopted son) says that the Indians call him Oglethorpe mico (or chief), and his words are good words, which they all believe.'

"'O he is my knight, without fear and without reproach!' cried out my youngest son; 'and my hero next to him is Christopher Columbus, for he discovered this goodly land, and Col. Oglethorpe is our Moses who has led us to it.'

"I have given you this conversation of my children, my dear friend, to show you their enthusiastic admiration for our Governor.

"Now, what remains for me to communicate? My letter has already grown to considerable length, so I will not go farther into the general information respecting the colony. I have told you nothing of our religious life or guidance. You may remember that the Rev. Samuel Quincey was our clergyman when last I wrote to you. He did not remain with us long. Although a native of the province of Massachusetts, he was educated in

England, and wished to return thither. So the 'Society for the Propagation of the Gospel in Foreign Parts' sent Mr. John Wesley as his successor. He was not unknown to me by birth and reputation, being a kinsman of the Earl of Anglesea, whose wife was a cousin of my mother's. Mr. Wesley's mother, Susanna Annesley by birth, was a particular favorite of the Countess of Anglesea, and I have heard of her superior virtues all my life. I have often thought of her wonderful cheerfulness and fortitude amidst great poverty and with so many children to train and minister unto. Her example, as I have heard of it, has been an encouragement to me when my path was dark and rough. Her husband, clergyman though he was, was also in jail for debt a short time once, and her heroic conduct under such trying circumstances was an inspiration to me through my time of similar trial; so there were many points of sympathy between us, although I had never seen her and she was very much my senior. You may fancy that I was pleased to learn her son was to be our curate—the very son who had been rescued from death when he was but six years of age, when their rectory was burned. We gave him and his brother Charles a warm welcome. The latter was the private secretary of Gov. Oglethorpe, and soon left for Frederica; but the former remained in our town, and we gladly offered him our hospitality.

We found him highly educated—in fact, a learned scholar—most earnest in his work, and eager to do good. His chief desire was to preach to the Indians; but, although they were friendly, and had great respect for Col. Oglethorpe, their desire for the knowledge that the white men could impart seemed to have abated. Tomo-Chichi himself admitted that they would not listen; and as the Spaniards and French were busily endeavoring to foment difficulties, it was plainly unwise for the good of the colony for Englishmen to go among them if unwelcome, or displease them in any way. But Mr. Wesley's hands were full while caring for his countrymen. His efforts did not cease with us, however, for he would preach to all who would listen, and learned foreign languages so as to communicate with those who spoke them. His peculiarly tender interest for the children won him their respect and love, and mine are inconsolable now for his absence, for he left last December. I would like to tell you the circumstances of his departure, but the mail in which this goes will close to-day, as the ship sails to-morrow; and if I were to begin I am quite sure I would leave the half untold. I can then, in but few words, say that they were painful circumstances. He was, I may say, the victim of misconception, injustice, and malice. While many friends felt sure of this, and deeply regretted it, yet he felt he could be more useful elsewhere, and else-

where he has gone. As I said, he returned to England in December, or rather he sailed then; perhaps he is still on the great deep. Wherever he
is, I pray God to bless him; for he has been a blessing to me and mine. If his life is spared, I am sure
he will do much good; for it certainly is his one
great desire to lead souls to Christ. Now that he
is gone, I love to worship with the Moravians.
Mr. Wesley loved them, enjoyed their services, and
declared that their elders, Spangenberg and Nitschmann, revealed the things of God to him. How
much more, then, do I need them to teach me; for,
my dear friend, the older I grow the more do I
'hunger and thirst after righteousness,' and I love
companionship that is sympathetic and can aid me
in my journey onward and upward.

"I trust your health is stronger. How warmly
would we welcome you to our table and fireside!
Perhaps a sea voyage might do for you what it did
for us. Is it quite beyond the bounds of possibility for you to visit us? My husband and each
child join me in this invitation, for your name is a
household word with us, and I have taught them
all to love you.

"Let me hear from you as soon as possible. If
you have heard or can hear of my family, please
inform me respecting them. With kindest regards
to your sister and her husband, I am as ever, my dear
friend, your affectionate   EVA WOODVILLE."

→CHAPTER VI.←

WE mentioned in a previous chapter that Mr. Wesley sailed from America for England on the 22d of December, 1737, reaching the shores of his native land on February 1st of the following year. The day before he disembarked the Rev. George Whitefield, his friend and co-laborer at Oxford, set sail for the New World, his destination being Savannah, and his intention and desire to preach the word of God in that place to all who would lend a listening ear. He was prompted to do so by a letter which Mr. Wesley had written not long before to his friends at Oxford, in which he had uttered a Macedonian cry, and called on them to "come over and help" him. "Who will rise up with me against the wicked? Whose spirit is moved within him to prepare himself for publishing glad tidings to those on whom the Sun of righteousness never yet arose? Only Delamotte is with me till God shall stir up the hearts of some of his servants, who, putting their lives in his hands, shall come over and help us where the harvest is so great and the laborers are so few. What if thou art the man, Mr. Whitefield? Do you ask what you shall have? Why, all you desire—food to eat, raiment to put on, a place where to lay your head, and a crown of life that fadeth not away."

His heart responded to the call; and leaving the

crowds that were flocking to hear him in England, and the rapidly increasing popularity that was afterward unprecedented, he determined to follow the impulse of his heart. He was but twenty-one years of age when, being ordained by Bishop Benson, he delivered his first sermon in the church where he had been baptized, and where he first received the sacrament of the Lord's Supper — St. Mary de Crypt, Gloucester. It caused much interest and excitement, which were increased by every succeeding sermon. While waiting three months in London before he embarked, he preached over one hundred sermons and collected above a thousand pounds for charity-schools and the poor.

All aglow with enthusiasm in his work, it need not surprise us that the long voyage to his new field of labor was used by him as a rare opportunity of reaching the hearts of all on shipboard. Touching at Gibraltar, a detachment of troops bound for the province were taken on; and now Mr. Whitefield rejoiced at being able to have access to those who so much needed his ministrations. Their commanding officer and the captain extended to him every courtesy, and he frequently preached and held religious services—his influence, so gentle yet effective, prevailing upon the soldiers to recite to him the Catechism as submissively as little children. Great must have been his joy when cards were displaced by Bibles, oaths exchanged for prayers, and many enlisted under the banner of the Captain of their salvation.

Upon arriving in Savannah he was cordially welcomed by the magistrates, and treated with marked respect. He continued the work that Mr. Wesley had begun—preaching, teaching at the various settlements, and visiting from house to house. He opened a girls' school in Savannah, and manifested great interest in the affairs of the colony.

Observation and reflection caused him to form the opinion that negro slavery was necessary to its prosperity. This conclusion was strengthened by greater familiarity with their condition; and in after years he successfully exerted his influence in obtaining a modification of the law which forbade the employment and ownership of African slaves.

Before leaving England the propriety of establishing an orphanage in Georgia had been suggested to him by the Rev Charles Wesley. Mr. Whitefield's philanthropy embraced the idea, and keeping it in view, upon his arrival in the colony he made suitable investigations, the result of which was a conviction on his part of the necessity for such an enterprise. Equally convinced was he that the funds required to accomplish the undertaking could not be raised on the western side of the Atlantic; therefore a visit to England became imperative for the success of his designs. Leaving Georgia, therefore, on September 6, 1738, he hasted, on his arrival, to lay his project before the trustees, who cheerfully bestowed upon him for his purpose a grant of five hundred acres. His eloquence now drew multitudes to hear him. Sometimes his audiences numbered twenty thousand souls. As many churches were closed against him, he preached in the open air, his ringing voice reaching almost a mile away, and the songs of praise from the vast concourse being heard twice as far. His ministries were among the collieries of Kingswood, on Kennington Common, Blackheath, and at Moorfield, to the illiterate and ignorant chiefly. Verily, the "poor had the gospel preached to them," and though the gentry and nobility were enraptured with his eloquence, still it was principally the "common people who heard him gladly"—that is, to the saving of their souls. He raised collections at the meetings, and such was his persuasive power that the fund for building his Georgia orphanage swelled to over one thousand pounds—large sums of this aggregate being often in half-pence, proving the generosity of his poorer listeners. Still being detained in England, he preached in various parts of the kingdom—how unweariedly, may be shown when we read the statement that in one week he preached not fewer than twenty-seven times. In August, 1739, he reëmbarked for the scene of his humane undertaking, encouraged with the hope of conducting it to a successful end.

Let us now return to Mr. Wesley as landing, as
we have said, on the morning of February 1, 1738,
he read prayers and preached at the inn; setting
out on his journey toward London after breakfast,
and reading prayers and expounding the Scriptures
in the little village where he spent the night: this
first day on the soil of England being indicative of
his future life, for, resuming his preaching in London the next Sunday, being then thirty-five years
old, he never ceased for the next fifty-three years,
unless he was seriously sick.   Then he "ceased at
once to work and live," leaving a memory fragrant
with good deeds, to which tributes of affection and
admiration were paid from the humblest collier or
lowliest cottager to the king upon his throne; for
George III. confessed that "to the Wesleys and
George Whitefield, and to the Countess of Huntingdon, the Church in this realm is more indebted than
to all others;" while in the light of later days unnumbered thousands agree with him who said,
"His life stands out in the history of the world un-
questionably preëminent in religious labors above
that of any other man since the apostolic age;" or
with the poet laureate Southey, who considered him
as "the most influential mind of the last century, the
man who will have produced the greatest effects
centuries hence."

But those preëminent labors had been but begun,
that influential mind had not reached its power, and

this special period of his life has been alluded to as his "transition" state; for, from doubts and heaviness he passed into such "joy in the Holy Ghost" as he had never before experienced—beginning with the memorable society meeting in Aldersgate Street, London, where, after three months of intimate association with Peter Böhler, the devout Moravian, and being led to understand the heights he might aspire to, he for himself experienced that whereof he had been taught, and "felt his heart strangely warmed," and continuing step by step till he reached the "full assurance of faith." Desiring to commune with others who enjoyed this blessing, he visited the settlement of the Moravians at Herrnhut in Germany. Amid their devout society he was so happy that he exclaimed, "I would gladly have spent my life here!" This remarkable town, which sprung into being because of the persecution following the preaching of the wonderful Christian David, was the cradle of the modern Moravian Church. David, the bush preacher, as his persecutors called him, was a zealous, indeed a fanatical, papist till twenty years of age, when he first saw the Bible, which then became his own book, leading him to renounce popery, and soon to begin to preach to his countrymen. His artless sermons were blessed to the conversion of great numbers who suffered cruel persecution because of their religious faith. He wearied not in his evangelistic

labors, carrying the first missionaries to Greenland,
and, poor carpenter though he was, on his way
preached to the court of the King of Denmark; visiting that distant shore twice again; going on his gospel
mission to Denmark, England, Holland, and eleven
times to Moravia. He also visited each Moravian
congregation within the limits of Germany, being
for thirty years an itinerant outdoor German
preacher. When not thus actively engaged, and at
his home in Herrnhut, he followed the example of
St. Paul, and by his hands ministered unto his necessities in that calling which should be endeared to
every Christian's heart, because it was that of the
Son of man. In 1751, at the age of sixty, he went
triumphantly home, to be "numbered with the
saints in glory everlasting." The doctrine which
this good man preached, and which produced such
glorious results, was *salvation by simple faith in
Christ.* No new doctrine in itself, thank God! yet
new to every soul that embraces it; and able, whenever and wherever preached, to save men of every
nation and every tongue.

How interesting is the fact that just at this junct-
ure in the world's great need this vital doctrine was
stressed as it had not been for generations! How
true it is that the Holy Spirit's power is limitless
and omnipresent! for revivals of religion began just
then in countries far apart, and holy men who honestly differed in minor points, yet alike in this, with

souls aflame with love to God, preached Christ crucified and faith in him to multitudes who flocked
to hear.   Not only were the labors of Christian
David blessed in Germany, but in America, just
before Wesley set sail for Georgia, a mighty work
began and continued for several years in New England.   The Rev. Jonathan Edwards "fanned the
fire into a holy flame." ˙ So many were converted—
high and low, rich and poor, moral and immoral;
so general were the meetings for prayer and the
songs of praise; so great the reverence, the meek-
ness, the charity—that this great divine said "the
New Jerusalem, in this respect, had begun to come
down from heaven, and perhaps never were more
of the prelibations of heaven's glory given upon
earth."   Simultaneously with these experiences in
America a reformation in Wales was brought about
through the instrumentality of Howell Harris, a
youth who, so happy in the love of God that he was
constrained to tell it to others, first visited from
h ouse to house, till, as the crowds gathered to hear,
almost unconsciously he began to preach, and finally
he would deliver from three to six sermons a day.
Clergy and magistrates threatened in vain, mobs
swore a nd stoned him, but like hundreds who were
to follow him, undauntedly he went on, till neighborhoods where drunkenness and licentiousness had
run riot were thoroughly reformed, and religion became the chief object of interest and conversation.

In Scotland also a wide-spread revival took place, beginning under the preaching of Mr. Robe. Soon in manse and school-house, in barn and field, prayer-meetings were held and happy converts shouted aloud God's praise.

And now we turn again to England, and mark the commencement of the great revival there. As we have seen, Mr. Whitefield had immense success in preaching to outdoor congregations which numbered many thousands, while he was waiting to sail for Georgia. His first open-air service was held February 17, 1739. Being denied the pulpit in the Bristol churches, he addressed two hundred colliers at Kingswood; the second service he spoke to two thousand people, their numbers next were four thousand, while at the fifth meeting the crowd was swollen to ten thousand; this in the bleak, cold months of February and March. For six months Mr. Whitefield preached in various places to these enormous gatherings till, wishing to visit more dis-tant points, he sent for Mr. Wesley and turned over to his care the vast congregations at Bristol and Kingswood. Mr. Wesley, whose labors had 'been for some months confined to cottages—as the church-doors were closed on him also as well as his brother —gladly answered the summons. Mr. Whitefield had crossed the ocean at his exhortation, and suc-ceeded him in his parish in the New World; now, in his turn, Mr. Wesley comes at his bidding to teach and confirm those committed to his charge. He now entered upon that limitless responsibility which he assumed when he uttered those memorable words, "I look upon all the world as my parish;" "the Lord giving him"—so wrote Mr. Whitefield, out of his loving, sweet spirit—"ten thousand times more success than he has given me."

These prominent examples were now followed by others. Field-preaching was fully established. The irregularity that caused the disapprobation of bishops and clergy, extending even to sermons of condemnation—that closed upon them the doors of churches, and encouraged mobs to hoot and stone and persecute—was fairly inaugurated. "What spirit is he of," asks Mr. Wesley, "who had rather these poor creatures should perish for lack of knowledge than that they should be saved, even by the exhortations of an itinerant preacher?" But the lay evangelists grew in numbers, and their fields of labor were multiplied till wherever a congregation could be had the truth of God was proclaimed: "Salvation by faith, preceded by repentance, and followed by holiness;" God owning and blessing the work by "adding daily to their number such as should be saved."

Among the colliers of Kingswood, who were notoriously ignorant and brutal, six weeks after Whitefield's first sermon to them the foundation-stone of a school was laid, they contributing twenty pounds

8

toward it. Soon after, a room was built in Bristol to contain the societies there—for gradually societies were being formed, bands organized, and the simple machinery of the future Church was beginning to move.

About this time, Mr. Wesley was requested to preach in a place that had been the Royal Foundry, but was then in a ruinous condition, because an explosion in the work over twenty years before had blown off the roof, shaken the walls, and killed and injured the workmen. He preached to seven or eight thousand people. The place was purchased, repaired, and modified for their peculiar needs. A large chapel, band-room, school-room, and preacher's house now occupied the spot where once the death-dealing instruments were made; and where men had toiled amid fire and smoke to prepare means to take their fellow-creatures' lives, now, amid prayer and praise, many who were once dead in trespasses and sins were made alive to God. This chapel was literally the cradle of London Methodism, and as their first house of worship possesses great interest to us.

Now, having seen the new-old faith fairly embarked on its career of prosperity—for Mr. Wesley maintained with perfect truth that it was the "plain old religion of the Church of England which was now almost everywhere spoken against under the *new* name of Methodism"—let us follow Mr. Whitefield on his second voyage to America, and note his endeavors in establishing the orphanage, whose success he had so much at heart. His friend Mr. James Habersham, one of the best and purest of men, who had accompanied him when first he came to Georgia, had during his absence located the grant of five hundred acres about ten miles from Savannah, and had begun to clear and stock the land. Some orphans had been collected and were accommodated in a hired house. On March 25, 1740, Mr. Whitefield laid the first brick of his Orphanhouse, which he called Bethesda—*i. e.*, "House of Mercy." He soon had forty orphans in his charge, and the number rapidly increased.

These were not half the number that depended upon him—some for support and others for payment of wages—for he had a large corps of workmen in his employ engaged on the new buildings, or cultivating the adjacent land. The responsibility was very great, and the need of large sums of money pressingly imperative. His purse was empty, but his heart was full of resolution and enthusiasm, while his fluent tongue was ready to pour forth its persuasive eloquence in his beloved cause. He visited Charleston first with much success, returning with money and supplies valued at five hundred pounds. He then proceeded to the northern provinces, more largely populated, older and richer than the struggling ones farther south.

Some interesting incidents are related of his visit to Philadelphia. One was of a gentleman who had previously to leaving home emptied his pockets because of his opinion that the house should have been located in that city, where were the workmen and materials for erecting it, instead of in Georgia, whither they had to be transported—yet, listening to Mr. Whitefield's matchless eloquence, became himself so *transported* that he turned to a friend requesting a loan wherewith to make a contribution to the collection which followed. The celebrated Ben Franklin, cool and unexcitable, resolving for the same reason that his purse should remain unopened, yielded to his magnetic influence by degrees—first deciding to give the copper in his pocket, soon including the silver, and ended by adding the gold. His ministry in Philadelphia produced a wonderful change in the inhabitants—from being indifferent about religion, their interest became so great that songs of praise were heard from residences on every street.

On this northern trip of a few months, he preached one hundred and seventy-five discourses, and collected in goods, provisions, and money more than seven hundred pounds. Transferring the business management of his enterprise to Mr. Habersham, and giving Mr. Jonathan Barber the charge of it religiously, he continued to do—after enjoying the Christmas holidays with them—what no one could do in his place—that is, raise funds for the continued support of the orphanage, until it should become self-supporting. Consistently with this duty he departed for England in January, 1741, and appealing for assistance in that kingdom, to Scotland, Ireland, America, and the Bermudas, he had the great satisfaction of receiving responses chiefly from the common people.

While the existence of the orphanage depended solely upon Whitefield's individual efforts, the disbursement of the funds and general management in the hands of Mr. Habersham were judiciously administered. The religious training of the children as well as their acquirements of mind and body were wisely attended to, and it became of great benefit to the colony, some influential, prominent, and useful citizens of Georgia having, in their youth, been partakers of this noble charity.

For many succeeding years, Mr. Whitefield's life was spent in England, where at the proper time we will speak of him again.

CHAPTER VII.

LETTER from Sir Edward Dudley, of Dudley Manor, county of Surrey, England, to Mrs. Eva Woodville, Savannah, in the province of Georgia, America:

"OCTOBER 5, 1739.

"*My daughter, my beloved daughter:* How shall
I address you?   After so many long, weary years
of cruel silence and neglect on my part, of patient
suffering and hope deferred on yours, shall I simply
call you my daughter once more, and say that I
forgive you?   Ah! if the dreary, long seasons could
roll backward, and if in reply to your first appeal
for pardon I now was writing, my words might be
few, my letter brief, and I might retain the dignity of the father who had been offended, but was
graciously pleased to condone your youth, and the
excessive trust in my leniency, and the imprudence
of your ardent lover's infatuation, all leading you
to disobey me for the first and only time in your
life.   But not now, my child, not now.   My displeasure has been far disproportioned to your offense.   I have heard of your trials and privations,
your sublime patience and heroic fortitude, and my
heart is broken because of you.   Ah, how differ-
ently does it all appear to me now!   How could I,
O how could I, cast off my own child, my only
daughter, my youngest born, my ever beloved and
lamented Ethel's dying-legacy?

"Surely I have proved the truth of the proverb
that 'pride goeth before destruction, and a haughty
spirit before a fall;' for by my hateful pride I
have caused the destruction of my peace of mind,
and the downfall of my own happiness for all these

weary years. Yes, it was pride, and pride alone—
the pride that I now see is 'an abomination to the
Lord,' but that I then thought was fitting and right
in my station in life. Even as I write these words
I loathe them, seeing that they and the ideas they
represent have blinded me to what was worthy and
estimable in character, unless a long line of ances-
try cast a fictitious glory around the unconscious
descendant.

"My daughter, I am a changed man now! I
feel as if a modification of the parable of the prod-
igal son might best describe my state of mind. I
have 'come to myself,' 't is true, at last; and now I
wish to come to my daughter and say unto her that
I have sinned against her and my Heavenly Father,
and humbly ask their forgiveness. I rejoice to say
that I feel that I have received his pardon for the
great and manifold sins of my life; and, my sweet
child, I am assured of yours—yea, even before you
tell me so. I can fancy the rapid throbbings of
your heart as you read my first address, and your
eyes swimming in tears as I abase myself before
you. I know you would silence me if you could,
and prevent my confession and humiliation; yet it
is a solace to me, and you must listen longer while
I tell you what brought about this change in me.

"I am getting to be an old man now, and my
eyesight is failing. I came to London a month ago
to consult an eminent oculist. Two weeks since I

was riding in my coach, caring not whither I was
driven so I obeyed my physician's order, which
was to take the air daily, when I found myself in
Moorfields. Why my coachman selected this direction instead of our usual drive in St. James's
Park I know not, but I have since had abundant
reason to thank God that he did so.

"Presently I found myself on the outskirts of a
crowd who were listening with rapt attention to a
sermon being preached by a small man neatly
dressed in clerical black. His manner was dignified and very calm, his tones clear and enunciation
so distinct that the vast throng heard plainly to its
outmost circle.

"Having no object in view in my drive, I bid the
coachman pause and listened to what he was saying.
You know, my child, that I have always been a
strict Churchman and regular attendant and com-
municant, so it never occurred to me that John
Wesley could have a message for *me*. To the ignorant and common rabble before me he might preach,
but in my mind I denounced the whole affair as a
'conventicle;' and in my fancied superiority to those
around me I felt that the needs of their souls was a
thing of which I knew and cared nothing. In my
proud contempt for them in their low estate, it was in
my heart to say, 'God, I thank thee that I am not as
they.' But as I idly listened with a careless curiosity,
to while away time which hung heavily upon me, I

heard words with which I had been familiar all my life, and yet, as he expounded them, seemed new and powerful as if spoken to me directly from heaven by God himself. 'Not every one that saith unto me, Lord, Lord, shall enter into the kingdom of heaven; but he that doeth the will of my Father which is in heaven.' As I listened I became more and more absorbed, and deeper conviction sunk into my heart. I felt that I had been saying, 'Lord, Lord,' without a shadow of a right to call him such, and that in justice he could say to me: 'I never knew you; depart from me, ye that work iniquity.'

"I did not hear the close of his sermon. If he showed the remedy after laying bare the disease, I know not. Doubtless he did; but my ears were closed to all around, and my whole consciousness absorbed in the new and terrible revelation. The service was over; the crowd dispersed; I drove silently home and spent a sleepless night.

"The next day I felt that I must hear that preacher again. My pride was so far lessened that although I had heretofore considered these field preachers as unworthy the countenance of orthodox Churchmen, yet I was now glad to learn that Wesley would hold a service that day in the old Royal Foundry. I went and heard a sermon from the text, 'If ye forgive not men their trespasses, neither will your Father forgive your trespasses.'

Then it was, my child, that I saw my unforgiving
conduct to you in a totally different light from that
in which I had viewed it for nearly twenty years.
I confess the struggle with my pride was great, but
finally God and the right triumphed; and pros-
trating myself, as it were, in the dust before him,
I felt assured of his pardon, not only by the flood
of love and light which illumined my soul, but by
the yearning tenderness which swept over me for
you and yours, and the desire to confess my over-
weening pride, and beg that the past should be
blotted out forever.

"I greatly desired to meet Mr. Wesley, and to
have conversation with him. Therefore, I sent my
coach for him, with a note requesting an interview,
little dreaming that by doing so I should learn your
place of residence and much concerning you.
Having forbidden your name to be mentioned in
my presence, I was in total ignorance of your history and locality, intending, however, that very
day to institute such inquiries as would lead to our
happy meeting, I trusted, in the near future.

"I will not undertake to give you a synopsis of
our conversation. It was to me beyond all value.
I believe in my new-found humility. I listened
like a little child as he 'expounded unto me the
way of God more perfectly.' And my faith grew
stronger, love deeper, and joy greater as he spoke.
I feel as if the new, beautiful hymn by Charles

Wesley, which his brother repeated to me, might have been written to describe my feelings:

> Tongue cannot express the sweet comfort and peace
> Of a soul in its earliest love!

I confessed to him how proud and unforgiving I had been, and this very humiliation was the immediate means of my learning at once all he could tell me concerning you. When I discovered that he had often been an inmate of your house when in America, that you belonged to his parish, and were on terms of intimate and affectionate friendship with each other, you may rest assured the questions I asked were neither few nor meager. By their means I learned the ages and sexes of your children, your present condition in all respects, and the trials and mortifications through which you have passed. Your patience, bravery, and Christian fortitude, while commanding my unbounded admiration, pierce my heart with anguish: for, while I had 'bread enough and to spare,' you almost 'perished with hunger.' Still worse: I, who should have nourished you in your time of need, refused the 'crumbs that fell from my table.'

"I will not dwell longer on this painful theme. Mr. Wesley tells me of your husband's energy and industry, of your thrift and prudence, and that your children are being trained in the same virtues. If I were a younger man, I should embark on the next ship, and as soon as wind and wave could transport me thither would embrace you; but I am not equal to such an undertaking. Moreover, my eyes demand continual treatment. So, Eva, my beloved, dare I proffer a request that would prove your loving forgiveness, and at the same time gladden my declining years as no other earthly blessing could? Can you not guess what is my desire? I feel a timid hesitancy in making it known, and yet I am strongly persuaded you will consent. It is nothing less than to pray you to give me your Ethel! Let her come now, so near the age you were when I saw you last. It is needless to say that no pains shall be spared in her education. As I am obliged to be in London a great deal, she will have the best advantages the metropolis can afford. The comfort and pleasure she will be to me words cannot express. Think it over, my dear Eva, and tell her father that while a large degree of selfishness certainly is in the proposal, I beg him also to consider the advantages to his child that the plan embraces.

"Your brothers were in fine health when I heard from them last. George is now in Parliament, and is a rising man. He is on the side of the Opposition, and one of William Pitt's warmest supporters. William is with his regiment in Spain. I hear troops have been sent from Gibraltar to Oglethorpe in Georgia. Possibly William may be among the number.

"I will now bid you farewell, my beloved child, earnestly hoping that I shall hear from you as early as practicable, and that your consent to my request will soon be followed by the sweet presence of your Ethel.

"I go now to call on the trustees of your colony in order to arrange to transmit to you in safety the sum of ten thousand pounds. Though too late for a marriage-portion, my dear, or in assisting you during so many years of your married life, I hope it is still in time to relieve you and your husband of much labor and anxious care. God bless you both and each one of your children, I pray from a full heart.

"Your affectionate father,

"EDWARD DUDLEY, BART."

A description of Eva Woodville's happiness upon the reception of the above letter would be simply impossible. For days she felt as if she were treading upon air, scarcely an idea or thought intruding itself but the joyful one that her father was reconciled to her once more. Little Annie could not understand her mother's profession of happiness, and the bursts of tears that followed every fresh perusal of the letter; for she felt like weeping at the suggestion it contained of her sister's leaving her; and in her one-sided view of the subject, she was ready to declare her regret that her grandfather had discovered their retreat, and remem-

bered them at all. Not so the boys. They knew
their mother's feelings better, and were glad to
have the load lifted from her heart. Besides, the
check for ten thousand pounds represented to them
exhaustless wealth. Even in those early days of
provincial simplicity, it was easy to adapt one's
plans and mode of life to an increase of income.
So they listened with eager interest to their parents
as they discussed the wisest manner in which to in-
vest their new fortune. As for Ethel, the letter
plunged her into a chaotic state of desires and regrets—aspirations for her new life and passionate
clingings to the old. She wished to plume her
wings for wider, higher flights, and yet was reluctant to leave the home-nest where she had been so
happy. At length her mother's attention was
drawn from her own position as daughter, and the
latter clauses of the letter claimed her attention.
The struggle was very sharp but brief, and she an-
nounced to husband and children that she saw her
duty clearly, and was glad to make amends to her
father by replacing, as it were, that treasure of
which she had deprived him years ago—a loving,
tender daughter, such as she knew Ethel would be.
"Herein will the demands of justice be met," she
said smilingly, while stroking Ethel's soft hair, the
tears gathering in her eyes, "and so tempered with
mercy," she continued; "for it is the best thing for
the child, and I am willing for her to go." Prepa-

rations for her journey were begun, but it was decided that she could not leave till the winds of March were over. Then she was delayed by a friend of her father's who was to be her protector on the journey. However, the time came all too soon for the parting; and with smiles all gone and streaming eyes, the mother and daughter bid each other farewell.

Letter from Ethel to her mother:

"Dudley Manor, July 3, 1740.

"*My beloved mother:* I can scarcely realize the distance that separates us; and yet methinks I should, when I call to mind the long, long voyage I took to come hither. But hearts can span time and space; and knowing how your thoughts dwell upon me, I turn my face to the west as I write, and feel as if yon setting sun could almost bear my messages of love to you, and tell you I am well and happy, yet long to see you. Yes, dear mother, I am happy, and very, very glad I am here. My dear grandfather—for I love him most tenderly already—so evidently enjoys my presence, his every look and tone evincing such deep affection for me, that I feel as if he *needed* me even more than you do, dear, sweet mother. Now, that is saying a great deal, is it not? But you have Annie, who is so amiable and thoughtful, and will soon fill my place —not altogether though, I hope; and Edward and Arthur are almost like daughters in their tender solicitude for your comfort; and dear father, who certainly "cherishes" you in the fullest sense of the word; while grandfather has no one but me. What a lonely life he must have led all these long years! What towering and deep-rooted pride he must have had to let himself be so lonely, when one word of love to you could have changed these silent halls into scenes of childish sports, and made them echo with our merry laughter!

"Although I read and re-read his letter to you, in order to form some idea of him before I came, and particularly dwelt upon his declaration that he was a changed man, I see now that the image I had formed of him was still in accordance with the one I had pictured all my life—a stern, haughty man, of whom I should stand in dread, and before whom I should be abashed and constrained. But O how mistaken I was! His mien is kingly. I am quite sure King George has not so royal a port. Does my Jacobite proclivities peep out there? My grandfather can no more change his dignified, majestic presence than he can the blood which courses through his veins, and of which he was once so proud that it wrecked his happiness. But beneath this grand exterior lies the humble spirit; and the kindly, gentle words to all, the patience, the calm, the peace, the heavenly peace which rests upon his brow, speak more eloquently than words of the change, to which every domestic in his service, every tenant on his land, as well as his neighbors and friends, all bear testimony.

"But I did not intend to begin my letter thus. I suppose I should first give you an account of my voyage. It differed but little from the one we all took together seven years ago. The accommodations for passengers were somewhat better, but my mattress upon the deck was far pleasanter than the cabin, and good Mr. Maxwell indulged me in my preference.

"I was friendly with all the passengers, and had it in my power to be of service to some. One dear old blind lady afforded me much happiness. I offered to read to her the first day that the seasickness left me, and never omitted till we landèd. I would read to her the lessons of the day, and one or two chapters besides; while she would sit by me, her head inclined to catch every word, her hand softly stroking and patting mine, her lips quivering with emotion, and such a look of rapture on her face that as I looked upon her sightless eyes upraised to heaven it seemed to me that though blind to earthly objects surely she saw even then the glories of the better world. Then her simple words of faith and joy, and her devout comments on the text, brought such a blessing to my soul each day that when she would thank me so gratefully for reading I felt that I should thank her for what she was doing for me. Sometimes I would

9

read her the beautiful hymns of Mr. Watts; and at last I brought out the dear old worn copy of 'Pilgrim's Progress' that I have loved since I was a little child, and for which, you know, I asked you as a companion book to my Bible, and the dearest link I could have to the days of my childhood when you read it to me first sitting on your lap, and from time to time, as your juvenile audience increased, heard it over and over, and never tired of it. More than any other object it is associated with each one of our home circle. I am glad my old friend had never heard it until I read it to her, for it is pleasant to feel she will always think of me in connection with it. She enjoyed it so much I read it to her twice during the voyage. It appeared to me as if her blindness helped her to see the wonderful incidents in Christian's pilgrimage more clearly than we can, just as Mr. Milton pictured the scenes in 'Paradise Lost' so vividly, for his mental and spiritual vision was brighter because of the lack in his natural eyesight. I wish you could have seen her face as I read of the Land of Beulah and the different pilgrims crossing the river Dear soul! I should like to be with her when she comes to its margin. I believe the waters will be very low, and she will go over almost dry-shod. She told me she would pray for me every day, dear mother; and I feel that I 'have entertained an angel unawares,' and my reward is very great.

"I spent much time too in helping a poor sick woman nurse her baby. He was very sprightly and active, and his bounds and leaps were too much for her strength. She protested he was an imposition on my kindness, but I really did enjoy the little fellow; and the look of relief and gratitude on her pale face as I would approach and hold out my arms for him to spring into was ample compensation for my trouble.

"'There were also several little children on board who seemed never happier than when they were gathered around me while I told them Bible stories, or read to them out of the Gospels; and remembering how you instructed us on our voyage to America years ago, I tried to recall your lessons of profit and of interest, and lead these children to thoughts of love and praise to God while beholding his wondrous works.

"You see, dear mother, my days were not allowed to hang heavily, and being so much occupied with others caused me to enjoy still more the hours when I could lie in silence and gaze up into the starry heights, or watch the long line of foam in the wake of our vessel, or the myriad sparkles in the restless waves, and think and gaze, and gaze and think, till finally I would see nothing that surrounded me, but before me would rise the dear faces of my loved ones and the familiar scenes of home. The blazing fire would shine upon you all—father with his book, and you at your swift spinning-wheel, the boys making their fish-nets or trap-triggers, little Annie frolicking with her kitten. Then the shifting scene would present a view of balmy morning. I could see you training and tying up your vines, Annie feeding her feathered pets, father and the boys busy afield, and so on scene after scene till presently I would struggle back into the present, and a feeling of loneliness would creep over me till I was fain to find forgetfulness in sleep.

"Few things of special note occurred on the voyage. Once we sighted a whale, and I watched him impatiently, fearing we should not approach him sufficiently near to see him spout; but we did, and I know not who enjoyed the sight most, I or my bevy of little friends.

"A brilliant aurora borealis delighted us one night, and a water-spout at some distance was an object of much interest; but on the whole it was an uneventful season, quiet and monotonous, and we landed safely at Gravesend, heartily glad to be on shore once more.

"My Uncle George met me, and was truly affectionate and kind. He declares I am your very image—that is, when you were of my age—and speaks of you with so much tenderness that it is hard for me to understand how he could have had so little communication with you through all these years. It is true he was on the Continent during the time of your greatest trials in London, but his letters since then have been few and far apart. I can only attribute it to two things—the natural antipathy most men have to friendly correspondence, and the fact that grandfather never would allow your name mentioned in his presence. The former reason I have no sympathy with, for I so dearly love to write to you; and the latter I consider no reason or excuse at all, but on the contrary should have made him desire closer intercourse with you. However, as I desire general amnesty, I am willing to 'bury the tomahawk,' 'smoke the calumet of peace,' and receive Uncle George's kind attentions in a gracious spirit; so do n't look grave at me, sweet mother—I am ready and anxious to love your relations as much as you desire I should, or as much as they will let me. Now, when that expression is applied to my grandfather it means a great deal, for I perceive already that he loves me dearly, and you know that is sufficient to win my affection. I have already made the acquaintance of all the domestics in this grand old house. With very few exceptions they are unchanged—the corps you left almost the same, with the exception of the aging effects of seventeen years. They remember you affectionately, and tell me many little incidents of your childhood, which I need not say interest me deeply.

"Your descriptions of this beautiful country-seat were so minute and vivid that I recognize it as a

spot I must have seen before. The effect upon me
is very strange and peculiar. Not only can I thread
the intricacies of the manor-house with precision,
but each path and terrace and woodland walk. As
I made my tour of discovery intentionally alone, to
see if I could accomplish it, and gallery, porch, and
turret, stair-way, chamber, and balcony, all presented themselves in proper order just where I expected them; and as my explorations extended to
the garden, lawn, and forest, and the shrubs, hedges, and grouping of trees seemed so familiar, I felt
that in some previous state of existence I must have
wandered here—that it could not be I was seeing it
all for the first time.

"I am very glad I was brought to Dudley Man-
or before going to London. I should have been
impatient to see your old home. As grandfather
does not expect to go to the city for some weeks, I
shall have an opportunity to thoroughly become
acquainted with this vicinity, for I wish to see and
speak with every one who formerly knew you. O
what a gossipy letter I shall write to you after that!
Then I wish to bring a little more brightness into
grandfather's life right here, where he has been sad
for so long.

"There is an indescribable air of gloom hanging
over the establishment, though neatness and order
are seen everywhere, and I wish to drive it away.
I feel that I must sing and be merry in these old

corridors and let in more of the blessed sunshine, in order to chase away the presiding genii of quiet and loneliness which have for so long held undisputed sway.

"This morning I was gathering flowers in the parterres in order to beautify the breakfast-table, and indeed the entire house—for they are blooming in great profusion now—and singing as joyously as the lark above my head. Suddenly grandfather appeared at the window just as I was singing Watts's sweet lines:

'My God, the spring of all my joys;'

and as I finished,

'Thou art my soul's bright morning-star,
And thou my rising sun,'

he spoke to me and smiled at my unconscious start of surprise. It was somewhat sooner than even his early hour, but I could not resist the fresh, tender charm of the morning, and once out-of-doors I could no more refrain from singing aloud my gratitude to the Giver of the beauty all around me than I could help inhaling the fragrance of the blossoms, or prevent the balmy, soft breezes from fanning my cheeks.

"'Your matin song called me to join you, my dear, and though my voice may not blend with yours, still I trust I can make "melody in my heart to the Lord;"' and as I approached him for a morning kiss, he patted my head and added: 'I do thank him for *this* gift to me. I hope you will be happy with your old grandfather, my love. I believe your presence will prolong my life.' With a sudden fresh access of affection for him, what could I do but assure him of it and of my deep content?

"Later in the day we went to church, it being Sunday, and heard a good sermon from the young curate, Mr. Lennox, who, I am glad to say, is very liberal in his views, and so devout and spiritually-minded that grandfather enjoys his sermons and long conversations. I found it hard to keep my thoughts from wandering, for it was the first time I had been in the church; and the recollection that there my dear mother was baptized as an unconscious infant, that there she assumed the vows made for her by her sponsors, was confirmed in the regular course, and Sunday after Sunday all through her youth joined in these same solemn words, and used the very book I held—for I saw your name traced therein—was more than my power of concentration could compass. I held my attention to the lessons and prayers, but confess I was not so successful during the sermon.

"In the afternoon grandfather asked me to go with him to the village, where he visited a few sick persons, speaking so gently to them, and to those who had gathered in their homes, of the claims of God upon them and the happiness of giving him

their hearts and feeling their sins forgiven, that the
tears gathered in my eyes. I felt then how changed
indeed he must be, to so humbly teach these lowly
cottagers what he himself had but recently learned.
They seemed deeply impressed, and I pray and believe his efforts will be greatly blessed. I told him
so as we were walking home through the fields, and
he replied: 'God grant it, my child; but when I
think of the long years in which I have done no
good to others, my heart aches, and I would be much
dejected if I had not resolved to put the past behind me—as my merciful God has blotted out its
sins—and now " press forward to the mark of my
high calling." I want to help others to see as I
now see, and to feel as I feel. I wish their eyes to
be opened to see what is so plainly set forth in
God's word, and yet which in my blindness I would
not see. Truly, having eyes I saw not, and having
ears I heard not. Mr. Wesley has been God's instrument in opening my eyes, and I wish to help
others as he has helped me.' Then he continued, dear mother, for some time to describe the
effect Mr. Wesley had on his immense congregations, and repeating portions of his impressive sermons.

"Grandfather never tires of dwelling on the
precious doctrines which the Wesleys, Mr. Whitefield, and their companions are reviving with so
much power. 'Some call them new doctrines,' he

said, 'and make this quotation from St. Paul: "If any man preach any other gospel unto you than that ye have received, let him be accursed;" and on this ground so many church doors have been closed to them. But this, you know, does not check them. I am glad they believe and act so as to show that while Church regulations are desirable for the perpetuation of Christianity, they are not vitally so, or that while the Church was established to serve Christianity, the converse of that proposition is not true. *New* doctrines, forsooth! New only as the sun might appear to a man who had been blind for a season. New only because of the indifference and irreligion which have for so long obscured the vision not only of individuals but of the nation. New? Nay, verily! rather they are as old as the words of Holy Inspiration; for Paul himself preached these very doctrines.

"'Is it justification by faith? What says Paul? "For by grace are ye saved through faith; and that not of yourselves; it is the gift of God."

"'Is it the witness of the Spirit? Hear Paul again: "The Spirit itself beareth witness with our spirit, that we are the children of God."

"'Is it holiness of life? Listen once more: "The very God of peace sanctify you wholly; and I pray God your whole spirit and soul and body be preserved blameless unto the coming of our Lord Jesus Christ;" then, as if human faith might stagger at such a height of attainment, he adds: " Faithful is he that calleth you, *who also will do it.*"

"'In another epistle, as if language fails to express the grandeur of privilege and duty to which we should aspire, he ascribes glory throughout all ages and world without end " unto him that is able to do exceeding abundantly *above all that we ask or think.*"

"'Do not these very cavilers, whenever the " Te Deum" is said or sung, use these words: " Vouchsafe, O Lord, to keep us this day without sin?" Is this an idle petition? If not, what does it mean? Do we ask God to do what we know he cannot accomplish? Or, if we believe he is able to keep us *this* day without sin, can he not keep us another and another and so on, till all the days of the years of our pilgrimage are ended? We are told that Enoch walked with God three hundred years. These years were composed of single days, and if we, with earnest faith, each day we live, pray this petition of the sublime "Te Deum," we may realize the truth of the glorious promise, "My grace is sufficient for thee."'

" You may know, dear mother, that this my first Sabbath in old England was a very happy day. I have been much interested in the prayers grandfather has held every night since my arrival, when he comments on the lesson, and adds a few words of exhortation and of extemporary prayer, so impressively that we all rise from our knees solemnized. But yesterday he so opened his heart to me, and conversed with me so familiarly, yet in a way to elevate and improve me, that I was flattered and humbled at the same time.

"When I go to London I hope I shall both see and hear dear Mr. Wesley. I am sure grandfather will have him frequently at our house. He says that Mr. Wesley spoke most kindly of our family, and was pleased to mention me specially, and that he had administered the right of confirmation to me in Savannah. Grandfather says his description of me convinced him that I would be a comfort to him. I promise you, mother, I will endeavor to be so. He asks me minutely of our life in Georgia. I have described our home and ordinary avocations, at the same time assuring him they will be considerably modified because of the present he sent you. He is anxious for the boys to be thoroughly educated, although their athletic sports and achievements in fishing and hunting interest him greatly. Some years ago he saw Tomo-Chichi and his party, who were brought to England by Gen. Oglethorpe, and my stock of incidents connected with him and the Indians of Yamacraw have served for his entertainment on several occasions. I gave him a particular account of his recent death, and endeavored to do justice to his character and the value of the services he has rendered our colony, as well as the many acts of personal kindness we, as a family, have received at his hands. I hope the monument Gen. Oglethorpe ordered to be placed over his grave will be speedily erected, for his name should be revered and remembered as long as our colony exists.

"Now, dear mother, it is time my lengthy epistle was being brought to a close. Please be as minute in every detail that interests you as I have been. I want to keep up my vivid realization of the daily life of each one of you until we meet again; for I assure you I look forward to the time when I shall persuade grandfather to take the voyage. Surely the time will become shorter, by means of improved appliances of navigation. When his eyes have been operated on, and he has recovered, doubtless a sea voyage will build him up as nothing else could. So 'Hope on, hope ever,' shall be my watch-word till I am in my beloved mother's arms once more. Tell father . .

"Your devoted daughter, ETHEL."

CHAPTER VIII.

LETTER from Mrs. Eva Woodville, Savannah, in Georgia, to her daughter Ethel, London, England:

"SEPTEMBER 15, 1742.

" Having given you such special details about each member of our family, and in fact all of our domestic arrangements, I must not close, my dear child, without informing you as to the state of the colony, more particularly as events of great importance have transpired since your last advices.

"Do you remember in 1739 how interested we all were in Gen. Oglethorpe's visit to Coweta town, three hundred miles from Savannah, where for two hundred miles his party met literally no one, and yet he pressed on through the unknown wilderness in order to meet the seven thousand warriors that were to assemble there, and to establish more firmly friendly relations with them? Do you not remember the graphic descriptions he gave us of the cordiality with which he was received, the hospitality they extended to him—even offering him that rare and choice drink called *foskey*, a decoction of the leaves and young shoots of the cassine or yapon, of which only their highest chiefs or 'beloved men' were allowed to partake? And do you not also recall the respect and affection with which his bravery, his fair-dealing, and consistent regard for his promises inspired them? It is evident that to this visit we have owed the peace and good-will which have surrounded us so long.

"Recently we have narrowly escaped a tremendous disaster. The Spaniards have been becoming more and more offensive and aggressive. The position our little province occupies, of being the breakwater, as it were, for the defense of the older colonies upon our north, is full of danger, and we know our borders are liable to be invaded by this foreign and relentless foe at any time. Last June occurred what will probably be known in our history as the affair of the Bloody Marsh, where Gen. Oglethorpe's forces, by means of a wisely planned and successfully executed ambuscade, and with very little loss, killed five hundred Spaniards. As this took place on our southern borders, the news was slow in reaching us. I had feared a collision, more particularly since your Uncle William arrived in Georgia with his regiment. I had not seen him, and felt myself more fearful for his safety, because I suppose he was so near, and yet we had not met. But soon after, the battle on St. Simon's Island took place, which by its brilliant victory caused the former achievement to sink into insignificance. The prospect for the defense of the island was unpromising— Gen. Oglethorpe's force was six to seven hundred men, the Spanish army numbered five thousand; his navy a few weak vessels, theirs a powerful fleet; yet such was his dash and bravery that acting on the offensive—as was his custom—he put their vast numbers to flight. With characteristic judgment and prudence he had with great rapidity caused a cut to be made through the marsh, which shortened the distance to Darien, and had provided boats to transport his men, in the event of the enemy push-

ing on vigorously against Frederica. Truly might
he say that obstacles and depressing circumstances
did not 'daunt but rather animated' him, for his
courage, forethought, and powers of resource appear
to rise with the occasion for them.

"It has been extremely gratifying to us all to
know in what high esteem Gen. Oglethorpe is held
in the other colonies, for he has received most cordial thanks for his successful defense from the
Governors of North Carolina, Virginia, Maryland,
Pennsylvania, New Jersey, and New York. Well
might they be grateful, for if our 'breakwater' had
not stood firm, a tide of hostile invasion might have
swept over them, to their great injury if not destruction.

"Gen. Oglethorpe has made his home on St.
Simon's Island. He sets an example of moderation
and simplicity, for no elaborate or costly mansion
calls him 'Master.' His pretty cottage, overshadowed by our fragrant forest-trees, has for its only
ornamentation graceful vines and flowering shrubs.
There, lulled to rest by the music of the rolling
waves which so lately beheld his supremacy over
his foes, or awakened by the sweet chorus of the
song-birds he loves so well, he enjoys a short repose
from the cares of his infant State or the fatigues of
the march and the battle-field. We hear he con-
templates a more decidedly aggressive movement,
and that ere many more months roll around he

proposes to march into the enemy's own domains and attack some point in Florida—most probably St. Augustine. If he does, I predict for him—victory! The prestige of his recent successes herald more to come. It has been said that they are unparalleled out of the Old Testament and the history of the ancient Jews.

"My brother succeeded in obtaining a furlough in order to pay me a visit, which, I assure you, we mutually enjoyed. The hot suns of Gibraltar and our own sea-coast have bronzed his bearded face so as to cause him to but slightly resemble the youth, fair and slender, I parted with so long ago. His gay spirits are unchanged. Edward and Arthur soon recognized in him a kindred spirit. A mutual love of adventure and sport led him to join them in the chase and similar pastimes, while for hours they would sit spell-bound as he would recount to them his experiences on land and sea, the strange sights and customs of foreign countries, or the hair-breadth escapes of himself or comrades from captivity or death. In return, our boys would entertain him with their store of Indian legends and traditions, exhibiting their hoarded wealth of relics from the Indian mounds they have explored. The short period of his visit passed all too soon, and he rejoined his regiment just previous to its sailing for England. Doubtless before this reaches you you will have met, and all that eager inquiries can

10

elicit of information and description concerning us will, I know, soon be yours.

"Next week Edward will leave us for Yale College. It seems a pity to separate the brothers who have never been apart a day in their lives; but Arthur is rather young to be sent so far away. His father prefers to have him remain under his tuition a year or two longer, and I cannot spare both at once.

"I am indeed glad to hear my dear father's eyes are steadily improving—tell him so with much love —and that you are progressing so well in your studies and music, and above all, my dear, that your soul is prospering. You are indeed greatly favored in hearing such spiritual preaching, and being so much in the company of the good, whose conversation must certainly be of great benefit to you. I thank you very much for the many sentences you send me of sermons you have heard and the beautiful new hymns. You remember how dearly I love those of Mr. Watts we have so often sung together. Now, those of Mr. Charles Wesley are becoming equally dear to me. I memorize them, and find in them great comfort and delight, particularly the one beginning,

O for a heart to praise my God!

How exquisite it is! I echo its every petition with all the earnestness of my being. O for a heart

Where only Christ is heard to speak,
Where Jesus reigns alone!

What more can we desire for time or eternity? I really believe Mr. Charles Wesley is doing as much for the world as his brother, for these beautiful little poems, embodying the purest Christian doctrine and the highest aspirations of the heart, are surely destined to be sung by millions yet unborn, and bear their spirits upward in communion with God, when the sermons of the latter are comparatively forgotten. Another hymn I much enjoy is:

> Forever here my rest shall be,
>   Close to thy bleeding side;
> This all my hope, and all my plea,
>   For me the Saviour died.
>
> My dying Saviour, and my God,
>   Fountain for guilt and sin,
> Sprinkle me ever with thy blood,
>   And *cleanse* and *keep me clean.*

Truly that is the essence of the prayer, 'Create in me a clean heart, O God; and renew a right spirit within me;' and 'wash me *thoroughly* from mine iniquity.' There is one line in another of the new hymns you have sent me that abides with me day after day. The hymn begins,

> O for a thousand tongues to sing
> My great Redeemer's praise!

and the line to which I refer is,

> *He breaks the power of canceled sin.*

My dear child, dwell upon the glorious thought.

Our sins are not only forgiven—canceled—but their
power can be broken, will be broken, *is* broken by
that Jesus whose name is 'music in the sinner's
ears.' Surely it does not require 'a thousand
tongues to sing the triumphs of such grace.' My
heart swells with adoring gratitude at such magnitude of mercy, and a new light is cast upon St.
Paul's declaration: 'Sin shall not have dominion
over you.' It is not only a command, it is also a
promise. It is an aspiration, justified, encouraged,
solicited by Him who is 'able to do more for us
than we can ask or think.' I find it a delightful
devotional exercise to trace in these new hymns
their perfect accord with gospel teachings, by
searching the Scriptures and collating correspond-
ing texts upon the subject. It seems almost incred-
ible that Christian pulpits should be denied to men
who preach such orthodox doctrines, and more
wonderful still that the Bishop of London should
have required the Wesley brothers in the beginning of their career to appear before him to answer
a complaint lodged against them to the effect that
they preached an absolute assurance of salvation.*

How strange that press and pulpit should unite
in denouncing that this doctrine was meant for all,
while some of their best and wisest ministers believed it was the privilege of only a few! I ob-

* Tyerman's Life of Wesley.

served what you wrote about Mrs. Susanna Wesley's father, Dr. Annesley, who declared that 'for forty years he had had no darkness, no doubt, no fear,' and yet that Mrs. Wesley could not remember to have heard him even once preach explicitly upon it. Herein I see the great advantage of the social meetings established by Mr. Wesley — the class and band meetings, the unreserved love-feast, and general encouragement for 'those that fear the Lord to speak often one to another.' If Dr. Annesley, for instance, had met his parishioners in similar meetings, the unrestrained recital of his experience might have been blessed far more than his sermons to the good of the souls of those to whom he ministered. In another of Mr. Wesley's hymns on this subject I read:

> His spirit answers to the blood,
> And tells me I am born of God.
>
> My God is reconciled,
>   His pard'ning voice I hear:
> He owns me for his child,
>   I can no longer fear:
> With confidence I now draw nigh,
> And Father, Abba, Father, cry.

These reminded me so pleasantly of Dr. Doddridge's lines:

> Come, sacred Spirit, seal thy name
>   On my expanding heart;
> And show that in Jehovah's grace
>   I share a filial part.

Cheered by a signal so divine,
Unwav'ring I believe:
Thou know'st I 'Abba, Father,' cry;
Nor can the sign deceive.

You remember our dear old Mr. Watts writes:

Dost thou not dwell in *all* thy saints,
And seal the heirs of heaven?

Truly it is pleasant to see that these good men,
differing though they may in many minor points,
so entirely coincide on vital questions. Listening
to the voice of the Master when he asks, 'How
readest thou?' they each take as a message to himself the word of St. John when he declares, 'He
that believeth on the Son of God hath the witness
in himself;' or St. Paul's affirmation: 'The Spirit
itself beareth witness with our spirit, that we are
the children of God. . And because ye are sons,
God hath sent forth the Spirit of his Son into your
hearts, crying, Abba, Father.' Continue to send
me the new hymns as they are published, dear
daughter. By thus doing you confer the highest
pleasure upon us all. Annie begs you to send the
music to which they are usually sung. She prac-
tices in a very systematic way, and, possessing a
decided talent, bids fair to become a proficient.
We have sweet seasons of sacred song every Sunday
evening, and at other times; and as your dear voice
cannot blend with ours, it will be pleasant to us to
know that we unite the same tunes to the hymns

we both use. All these pleasant incidents, small though they may be, combine to enhance the sweet preciousness of that communion of saints which to us, my beloved first-born child, has never been a mere formal, creed-like utterance, but a living, loving delight. Thank God for the faith by 'which we meet around one common mercy-seat,' a foretaste of that heaven to which, I trust, we are tending.

"Now, dear daughter, I must indeed cease, with renewed assurances of love from each one of our circle to our absent lamb. YOUR MOTHER."

⇢ CHAPTER IX. ⇠

LETTER from Ethel Woodville to her mother:

"LONDON, January 1, 1743.

"*Dearest mother:* Your letter has just been received. A sweet New-year's gift! I will begin my reply before the day is over, so that literally I can offer you New-year's greetings. My thoughts have rested on you continually for the past two weeks. My fancy depicted you busy in your preparations for Christmas cheer, with Annie your willing assistant. I doubt not she is a notable little house-keeper, being now in her fifteenth year. Her letters show plainly how rapidly her literary education is progressing; while, thanks to your judicious care and the necessities of our colonial life, Annie's skill in domestic accomplishments will cause me, I much suspect, to look to my laurels in that line. This reminds me to thank you for the various preparations of Indian corn I have lately enjoyed. The sacks came safely, and I observed that dear father had taken great pains to gratify my whim, the grains of corn being so large and white. You remember my reason for requesting that a few bushels be sent over to us was that grandfather had expressed a desire to taste the dishes in whose praise I had spoken. Last spring, when the seed-corn for which I had written arrived, I requested the gardener to pay special attention to its planting and cultivation. The result was such a beautiful patch of maize that it challenged the admiration of the neighborhood. Visitors requested to be allowed to see the luxuriant tropical growth, and I was asked to reserve seed by ladies who desired stalks to ornament the choicest portions of their grounds. When the ears were in proper condition, you may fancy the pains I took to have them properly roasted or boiled for my grandfather's first essay in eating green Indian corn. He approved them fully as much as I desired he should; and it was owing to his expressed curiosity in regard to the articles of food made from the fully ripened and dried grain that prompted me to ask father to send me some in quantity. Tell him he would have been much amused at the anxious solicitude with which I superintended the operations of the miller as he

ground some of it into flour * and some into hominy. We were at Dudley Manor when it arrived.
The old miller and I are special friends. With
most obliging alacrity he changed and graduated
his stones to produce the desired results. I also
had made under my directions a large wooden
mortar and pestle, such as we use in Georgia to
prepare the large hominy which is one of your
favorite dishes. I even had a little of the genuine
Indian dish *sofky* prepared, the entire corps of domestics looking on the while with amused curiosity.
When my material was ready, with my own hands I
soon prepared each variety for our table, and had the
satisfaction of seeing that disuse of my kitchen accomplishments had not resulted in forgetfulness or
loss of skill. The steaming hot, snow-white hominy was decidedly a new sensation. Grandfather
tasted, smiled, and finally made it his breakfast.
The next morning my pan of rich, porous egg-
bread and light, melting batter-cakes vied with
each other in his favor; but when with an air of
complaisance I set before him my dishes of *sofky*
and large hominy, feeling that my cookery would always secure his approbation, I was speedily unde-
ceived, as, with a shake of his head and a wave of
his hand, he motioned Tompkins to remove his
plate, one taste of its contents being quite sufficient.

---

* On the sea-coast of the Southern States corn-meal is
generally spoken of as *corn-flour.*

"Grandfather's health is very fine. It is hard to realize that he has entered his seventy-fourth year. His eyes are also improving; he is able to read every day. He told me to-day that he had finally decided he could not attempt the sea voyage to America. Ever since I have been with him, to my urgent appeals on the subject he has postponed a decision, still leaving me hope to cheer me for the future. I had hardly time this morning to feel the force of the disappointment, when he added that he had written to you to come over to see him, and for father and all your children to accompany you; 'for,' he continued, 'I feel like ancient Jacob when he beheld his long-lost Joseph. If I can but see her face once more, I shall be ready to say, "Now let me die."'

"Now, dear mother, I feel as though the winds and waves cannot bring you to me soon enough. O the long, long weeks ere this will reach you, and then the long, long weeks ere you can reach us! I will pray God to send prosperous gales, and grant you a safe and speedy journey. I beg you not to delay to answer our letters. Come 'by return mail,' as it were. I trust dear father will arrange at once to leave his home and business—for one year at least—and come over. I am quite sure he wishes to see his aged parents. Grandfather told me he would arrange so that no loss should accrue to him because of his absence from his estates. But why

need I multiply words, dear mother? I am sure
you will come as soon as possible, now that the expectation of a visit from us is at an end. I will
take note of the time, and look for you and all my
dear ones as soon as it is practicable for you to arrive.

"My pen runs away with me so when I write to
you, dear mother, that I will curb it before it begins on trifles again, and tell you of the watch-
night meeting we attended at the Foundry last
night. The large building was full to overflowing.
We had a solemn, heart-searching discourse from
Mr. John Wesley; then a season of prayer and
song. As the hour of midnight drew near, we
were exhorted to review our experience of the past
year, to repent in all humility for our misdeeds
during its course, and to renew our covenant with
God. Then we sung Mr. Charles Wesley's hymn:

> Come, let us use the grace divine,
> And all, with one accord,
> In a perpetual cov'nant join
> Ourselves to Christ the Lord.

Dear mother, I wish you could have heard the volume of sound that rose from that vast concourse. It
seemed that every voice echoed the aspiration of
every heart as each verse of the hymn was sung in
a joyous abandonment of consecration that declared
a happiness earth can never give. As we sung the
lines,

> And if thou art well pleased to hear,
> Come down, and meet us now!

the blessing came. The answer was instantaneous. I realized what it must have been on the day of Pentecost, when 'suddenly there came a sound from heaven as of a rushing, mighty wind, and it filled all the house where they were sitting.' Surely no one in that company who participated in that joy—and it seemed to me there was no exception—can ever forget it, can ever doubt the witness of the Spirit, or that our bodies can be the 'temples for the indwelling of the Holy Ghost.' As the last vibration died away, after we had fervently sung the closing lines,

> And register our names on high,
> And keep us to that day,

we knelt for silent, private prayer. In that solemn, holy hush, God only knows the depth and ardor of the vows of which the recording angel took note. Directly the slow strokes for the midnight hour warned us that another mile-stone of our life was passed, and in a few moments more a voice tremulous with emotion broke the silence—a voice which, as confession changed to supplication, to thanksgiving, to adoration, grew stronger and more clear, till its closing triumphal ring was a fitting vehicle with which he called on every thing that had breath to praise the Lord. The song which followed was a trumpet-call to unwearied service and joyful duty:

> Come, let us anew our journey pursue.

We sung the last verse:

> O that each in the day of his coming may say,
>   'I have fought my way through;
> I have finished the work thou didst give me to do!'
> O that each from his Lord may receive the glad word,
>   'Well and faithfully done!
> Enter thou into my joy, and sit down on my throne.'

We bowed our heads and hearts while the sweet words of the glorious benediction rested like music from heaven upon our ears: 'The grace of our Lord Jesus Christ, and the love of God, and the communion of the Holy Spirit, be with us all evermore. Amen.' We went out into the quiet night with that blessed grace and love and communion within us, and felt that it was but a step from earth to heaven; felt that neither height, nor depth, nor any other creature, could separate us from the love of God; felt that we could count it all joy to suffer for his sake. Alas! dear mother, some of our little band do suffer for his sake. One has already won a martyr's crown. When I mention his name you will recollect him, I am sure, for it is no other than William Seward, who was Mr. Whitefield's traveling companion in his second voyage to Georgia. He was killed in Wales, where he was itinerating with Howell Harris, of whom I wrote you as being the chief instrument in the recent great revival in that country. They were both treated with extreme rudeness in many places; at last it became cruelty. They were pelted with stones and dirt. On one occasion Mr. Seward's eye was struck, which caused him to lose the sight. Soon after, he received a violent blow upon the head which proved fatal.

"So far this is the only death by martyrdom among our number, but the insults and outrages far exceed my power to describe. Sometimes the preachers are assailed by the mob with a deluge of filthy water, dead cats and dogs are thrown at them, they are pelted with any missile that can be obtained, or they are ducked in adjacent ponds; fire-rockets are thrown into the congregations, beasts are driven amongst them, bells are rung, trumpets are blown, and every imaginable device is resorted to to distract the attention of the people and force them to disperse. This malicious treatment extends even to the dead; for but a few days ago a funeral procession was assailed, and dirt and stones were thrown. This mode of persecution is not confined to the lay preachers and exhorters, but Mr. Whitefield himself and even the Messrs. Wesley receive the same treatment. Mr. Charles recently suffered the indignity of having his nose pulled, while his brother endured a blow between the eyes from a stone while preaching, which, however, did not silence him, for, wiping away the blood, he continued his discourse. I suppose there has been no greater or more violent mob than at

the preaching of John Cennick. He is the author
of the hymn I inclose,

Children of the Heavenly King,

and is the first lay preacher in the kingdom. His
experience is very interesting—such depth of conviction and humiliation, and after his conversion
such devotion, such abundant and successful labors!
In molesting him the mob appeared almost frantic.
They used a fire-engine to drench the congregation
with water; guns were fired over their heads,
drums and tin-pans were beaten, and cudgels used
with cruel malignity. Such demonstrations are
chiefly made in country neighborhoods and the
outlying districts and towns, for the preachers are
itinerating all over the kingdom. Mr. Wesley is
journeying through Northern England, and in
spite of opposition he is most successfully establishing societies in many places. In the year just
past the society in Newcastle, founded only a few
months ago, has grown to eight hundred members.

"I must not fail to tell you of an interesting incident in Mr. Wesley's visit to Epworth, which was
his father's parish, and where at one time of his life
he had assisted him for awhile. But now the pulpit, from which he had then preached, was denied
him, so taking his stand on his father's tombstone,
in the quiet of the evening hours of the Lord's-day,
he preached to the largest congregation the village

had ever seen. For eight days the scene was repeated, and each meeting was one of great power and blessing. Mr. Wesley, in speaking of his visit there, remarked that 'for near forty years his father labored there and saw but little fruit of his labor; that he also had taken pains with them, apparently in vain, but now the seed sown so long ago sprung up and brought forth fruits meet for repentance;' and added, 'Let none think his labor of love is lost, because the fruit does not immediately appear.' Only think, dear mother, what his feelings must have been, as standing over his father's grave, denied admittance to that father's former pulpit, his thoughts reverted to the days of his childhood, his immature youth, his riper years, up to the present time, when in the heat and burden of the day he is engaged in this hand-to-hand conflict with sin and Satan and the powers of darkness. The circumstances were calculated to quicken the tenderest recollections of the love and faithfulness of that aged mother who was so soon to go before him into the 'place prepared' for her in the 'many mansions.' For some time past she had been living in the preacher's residence attached to the Foundry when it was remodeled into a chapel. Here she could be more frequently with her son, to receive his filial care and assist him with her affectionate advice and sympathy. It was owing to her judgment that Mr. Wesley admitted lay preachers into his new organization. At first he was much opposed to it, till convinced by her wisdom, and seeing that God acknowledged their labors most signally, he felt as did Peter when, making his defense before his brethren at Jerusalem for having baptized the household of Cornelius, he said: 'Forasmuch then as God gave them the like gift as he did unto us, what was I that I could withstand God?' And truly, if God's Spirit rests upon his messengers, how much greater is that qualification than any learning the universities can bestow! Did not God call Elisha from his plow and Amos from his herds? Did not Peter and Andrew, James and John, leave their fishing-nets, and Matthew his tax accounts, when Jesus said, 'Follow me?' And was not their commission as truly divine as Isaiah's or Daniel's, as Luke's or Paul's? Cannot the promise of old made to Moses be renewed to those whose hearts are right in the sight of God: 'Go, and I will be with thy mouth, and teach thee what thou shalt say?' Moreover, surely all who feel the responsibility of being embassadors for God, and the language of whose hearts is, 'Who is sufficient for these things?' will endeavor to improve the talents of their minds as well as their hearts, will regard Paul's advice to Timothy and 'give attendance to reading,' so that they may become 'apt to teach,' and be '*thoroughly furnished* unto all good works.'

"Grandfather says a most prominent feature of

11

this great religious work is the fact that the 'poor
have the gospel preached to them.' It is true
they can hear a sermon and the prayers every Sunday in the parish church, but there, as a general
thing, the 'word of life is not rightly divided unto
them.' They are too illiterate to understand the
tropes and similes, the rounded periods and classic
allusions, which in most cases would not benefit
their souls if they could, and it is to them like
worshiping in an unknown tongue. The reason the
'common people' hear gladly the so-called Methodist preachers is that they speak from the heart to
the heart, and while plainly proclaiming the righteous law of God, they show their hearers wherein
they have offended against this law; then holding
up the cross of Christ as the only plea for pardon,
they teach them that it is their blessed privilege to
know that their sins are forgiven by the indwelling
of God's Holy Spirit. They encourage mourners
for sin with narrations of their own experience and
that of others, as Mr. Charles Wesley sings:

> What we have felt and seen,
>   With confidence we tell;
> And publish to the sons of men
>   The signs infallible.

Their language being adapted to the capacity of
the bulk of their congregations, their interest is
aroused and riveted at every service. These last
few thoughts, dear mother, I confess are reproduced

from a conversation I have lately had with Mr.
Lennox, the curate of our parish at Dudley Manor.
He sympathizes thoroughly with this new movement, and his sermons reflect his convictions. His
efforts for the spiritual improvement of his parishioners, supplemented by grandfather's wise and liberal coöperation, have resulted most successfully.
Godliness is established in many hearts, cleanliness
and thrift rule their dwellings, and I think there
can be no happier cottagers than those who crowd
our village church and school, or gather around
their beloved Squire, as they evidently regard grandfather. Indeed, he moves among them like a patri-
arch, a model landlord, solicitous for their souls and
bodies, taking an interest in all and each, and deriv-
ing unalloyed happiness by doing so. He declares
his last days are certainly his happiest, as he trusts
they are his best.

" But I have made a long digression. I will return to the subject of Mrs. Wesley's living in the
Foundry, by remarking how fitting it was that she
should do so, and also how appropriate that she
should from this spot, where was the incipient organization of that branch of the Church on earth
her son had founded, take her flight to the Church
in heaven. Her end was peaceful—no clouds, no
doubts or fears. To depart and be with Christ
was all her desire. Mr. Wesley and five of her
daughters witnessed her painless, peaceful death.

and obeyed her dying-request, which was: 'Children, as I am released sing a hymn of praise to God.' *Released!* How much meaning in that word! Released from doubts and fears, from inward conflicts and outer temptations, from misconstructions and misconceptions, from timid hope, from faltering faith, from waning love, and ushered into an eternity of *satisfaction*, having *awaked in His likeness.*

"I have written far into the night, dear mother. I opened my window just now to look out, and the myriad stars appeared so far away, and this earth so small, so insignificant, I felt like an atom on its surface. Then I remembered that the heavens were the work of His hands who also counts the hairs of my head, and a sweet sense of his protection came over me; and I will now lie down to rest, committing you and all my dear ones to his keeping as fully as I say for myself: 'I will both lay me down in peace and sleep, for thou, Lord, only makest me dwell in safety.'

"Your loving child,   ETHEL."

⇢CHAPTER X.⇠

LETTER from Mrs. Eva Woodville, of Savannah, in Georgia, to her daughter Mrs. Ethel Lennox, of Dudley:

"January 1, 1754.

"*My dear daughter:* It did not need the over-looking of packages of letters received from you years since to prompt my writing to you to-day. It is simply in accord with our unvarying custom to do so on every anniversary of any note throughout the year. I am well assured that before you seek your pillow this night you will find time to send to me New-year greetings, as I do now to you and yours— your good husband and those three darling children I so long to see. May the good Lord make this year one of special blessing to you, I pray.!

"I referred to my looking over a package of your old letters. I frequently do it, my dear; it is an inexpressible pleasure to me. This morning I felt like indulging myself in that way, and have just finished reading the last one received from you be-fore my departure on my visit to England eleven years ago. It possesses particular interest for me, for it is the last one in which my dear father's liv-ing presence is alluded to. How thankful shall I ever be that in prompt response to his letter of the same date I made him the visit he desired! Fondly does my memory revert to those happy, tranquil months we enjoyed together when, in his vigorous, beautiful old age, he illustrated such Christian graces as we should strive with our best energies to imitate. When the summons came suddenly and with but little warning, how joyfully he heard it!

We rejoiced that his exit, while painless and short, was long enough for him to show us how triumphantly a Christian could die—heaven's gates seeming to open so wide for him that, as in the case mentioned in our dear old 'Pilgrim's Progress,' the glory almost shone upon us. How could we lament and mourn for one so blessed, and yet how sorely did we miss him!

"Another fact, dear Ethel, makes that letter precious to me. It is the last, you remember, I received from you as Ethel Woodville. Ah, what a gratification it was to me to be with you at your marriage! The necessary preparations for it drew off my mind from dwelling too steadily upon my bereavement after my father's death; while becoming well acquainted with your chosen one, and feeling that I could intrust you willingly to his manly, tender love, acted as a balm to the fresh wound caused by a continued separation from you. Yours has been a well-assorted marriage, my dear child, and I can truly say I would rather see you the wife of Thomas Lennox—faithful pastor, devoted Christian, affectionate husband and father that he is, although the humble curate of a country parish—than the titled mistress of the finest estate in England, with circumstances calculated to act as hinderances and not helps on your journey to heaven.

"The few months I remained with you after your marriage were sufficient to show me you had made no mistake in electing your life's work. As your husband's faithful companion, coöperating with him in all his endeavors to elevate his flock, as the friend of each parishioner, as the teacher of the little ones, you proved yourself a helpmeet for the former, an exemplar for the latter, and a blessing to all. I was glad also to welcome my new sister—your Uncle George's bride — to Dudley Manor. Though late in life to give up his bachelorhood, he really waited to purpose, for his young wife was as beautiful as she is amiable, as clever and cultivated in mind as winning in disposition, while really George was so youthful in appearance none would have guessed that he was near fifty years of age. It would have been sad to have the old hall uninhabited, except for his occasional visits; but now it is pleasant to think of it as the seat of hospitality and happiness, for Alice, with her domestic tastes and joyousness, will always diffuse brightness around her. I am glad you find her so congenial, and that your little children and hers will grow up in intimate, affectionate relations, as kindred should.

"Well, ten years have passed since that visit, yet I can still picture you all as I saw you then, with the addition of the 'little olive-branches around your table'—your twin boys, Dudley and Woodville, and my own little namesake, Eva. Your frequent letters and minute descriptions of their actions and sayings bring them very vividly before me. I am living over my younger life again in that of my children; for with my ten grandchildren I sometimes think that I ought to feel quite far on the shady side of life. Your father, however, insists that I bear my fifty years with wonderful ease and youthfulness; and truly my health is so good, my spirits so equable, I have so much to be thankful for, and am so blessed and happy, that I cannot feel old.

"Your brother Edward continues to practice law with marked success. His ambition and determination are so great that I really believe even if he had been debarred the great advantages he has enjoyed, at Yale College, he would still have ranked high in his profession. He is very studious and diligent, and really the first lawyer of his age in the colony. He has built a large and handsome house fronting on Oglethorpe Square, and his little boys, Habersham and Whitefield, are growing finely. Arthur's head-quarters are still with us, but his wife objects so much to his long and frequent visits to his plantation fifteen miles up the river that he is building a residence there, and will remove in a few weeks. He calls his place 'Tomo-Chichi,' in honor of his old friend. His children afford us so much pleasure it will be hard to part with them, little Maxwell being his grandfather's shadow; but we shall expect to see them often.

"While so many will leave the home-nest, I trust

I may not have to be separated from Annie. Her husband, being a physician, will certainly remain in the town, paying only occasional visits to his plantation, which adjoins ours, only five miles away. I think I should be obliged to enter a decided protest if her darling cherub were removed from my roof.

"Great changes have been made in our colony since the extension of the land tenures to absolute inheritance and the introduction of slavery five years ago. Now that persons can hold their land in fee-simple, and secure laborers who are unaffected by the climatic influences that so often prove injurious to white residents, the entire province has received an impetus to an enlarged prosperity that bids fair to be permanent. Often have we been discouraged by the languishing condition of public affairs; but now, under the operation of these two wise conditions—for which we frequently petitioned in vain—our hope and energy took on a new growth, and success has been and still is crowning our labors. I feel very keenly my responsibility in regard to these heathen, and firmly believe we will be guilty in the sight of God if we fail to instruct them in his law, and tell them of the offers of gospel grace. I express my sentiments freely on the subject, and try to influence others to view it as I do. Arthur and his wife quite agree with me, and the latter declares her intention of following my example as soon as she removes to their plantation, by reading, instructing, and conversing with them on the subject of religion. I drive out for this purpose every Sunday afternoon, and am gratified by increased attention and interest on their part. Surely it is better for them to be brought hither to a land of civilization and gospel light than to remain in a far worse bondage on their native soil. Granted that this is not the object of their being transported here; that some of them are torn from parents or wives and children; that the voyage is a source of great discomfort, perchance of misery, to some; that their owners in this country may be exacting or unkind; and after considering all these points, I still reply, It is better for them as a class to be brought to America. Bondage there is far more bitter than it can possibly be here, for laws humane and prudential guard their welfare here, while tortures and death at the whim of a cruel, absolute despot may be their portion there. The vast majority were rescued from a fate worse than death, having been captured by their foes and awaiting their summons to be offered as sacrifices to a blood-thirsty and rapacious idol, or as a holocaust on the tomb of a dead tyrant. The other objections are grave indeed, but, while much can be said on both sides, this is not the time or place to present them. Slaves will be brought in now, however, in large numbers;

for the prohibition was raised, you know, in 1749, and two years ago, when the trustees of this Georgian province surrendered it to the Crown, and it was placed in charge of the Lord Commissioners for Trade and Plantations, the slaves numbered one thousand and sixty-six, while the white population was two thousand three hundred and eighty-one. This estimate did not include troops or boatmen. Neither was counted in a congregation recently from South Carolina, now settled on Midway River. Of this settlement I think I have never told you. They have been a long while in realizing their 'Alabama.' As far back as 1630 they sailed from Plymouth, England, for this New World. A company of Puritans gathered from Devan, Dorset, and Somersetshire. They founded Dorchester, Massachusetts, but hearing of the sunny land farther south, where rich lowlands requited the toiler more freely than the stony coast they inhabited, and where frozen streams and snow-clad hills were unknown, in 1695 they removed to South Carolina, and on the banks of the Ashley River, eighteen miles above Charleston, they began a settlement, named for the one they had left, and which had been their home for over fifty years. Devout and united, they brought with them their pastor, Rev. Joseph Lord—let the names of good men be remembered—and hoped they had found an abiding-place. And so that generation had, and the next; but in course of time, the lands being impoverished, and much sickness prevailing, their descendants concluded to migrate again. The dissatisfied flock began to search for new pastures, and two years ago, accompanied by their beloved shepherd, the Rev. Mr. Osgood, they purchased lands on Midway River, some forty miles from Savannah, and moved without delay. They numbered three hundred whites and fifteen hundred slaves—a sober, worthy, industrious people, an acquisition to any colony who desire a God-fearing population.* That this has been the earnest wish of our founders—the board of trustees—to whose wise counsels and intelligent interest in our affairs we are so much indebted, no one can doubt. They have made every effort to supply us with religious teach-

---

*This settlement was the origin—the nucleus—of Liberty county, one of the choicest counties in the State, from which has emanated a savor of virtue, refinement, and religion, whose influence will go down the ages in increasing power. Nearly fifty ministers of the Presbyterian Church claim this as their native county, while many noble sons have illustrated her on the battle-field and in every peaceful walk in life. The historic Midway Church, originally built of logs, echoed to the first sermon on June 7, 1754. The tenderest recollections of those who once worshiped there will ever linger around it. In 1758 the town of Sunbury was begun. Once it bid fair, in its rapid prosperity, to rival Savannah; but long since it has been numbered among the "dead towns" of our Commonwealth.

ers, and we have had earnest and faithful preaching from many who desired to do us good. It was indeed a day of thanksgiving to this parish when our new edifice, 'Christchurch,' was completed July 7, 1750. I have written you of it, I well remember, but by my letter you see I am in a retrospective mood. It is somewhat remarkable—is it not?—that this is the only parish of which Mr. Wesley and Whitefield were ever rectors, for in their subsequent itinerant life they have had no other.

"I trust the management of the colony under our new and first royal chief executive—Gov. Reynolds—will be as competent as it has hitherto been. I hope the qualities of firmness and promptitude of action in time of emergency are possessed by him, for these are most necessary qualifications in one occupying his position. I shudder even now to think what might have been the result that fearful day in July over six years ago if our brave President Stephens had shown less resolution. When Bosomworth and his wife—the latter interpreter between Gen. Oglethorpe and Tomo-Chichi long years ago; the Mary Musgrove of your early recollections—accompanied by Malatche, the King of the Creeks, who in his ignorant fanaticism was a pliant tool in her hands, and willing at her bidding to abdicate in her favor, were escorted by hundreds of fierce warriors who, making hostile demonstrations, demanded that their 'queen,' as they called her,

should be reinstated in her rights, nothing short of
heroic firmness and presence of mind could have
saved us from bloodshed. As the women and children trembled at home, our men patrolling the
streets, the military being ordered out, we still felt
a strong conviction that Mr. Stephens would overcome the excited Indians, and influence them to
leave us without an attack. What relief we felt
when they retired, leaving the unprincipled woman
who caused the disturbance in temporary detention! Her claim of five thousand pounds and the
islands of St. Catherine, Ossabaw, and Sapelo is
certainly unreasonable, but a portion of it should
be awarded her, and no doubt will be.

"I frequently have the pleasure of listening to
dear Mr. Whitefield's persuasive eloquence. How
can any one hear him unmoved? He comes back
and forth from England to America on his mission
of mercy, for he continues much interested in his
school at Bethesda, yet wherever he goes preaches
with a frequency and power as if no other object
could occupy his thoughts. As he says, he believes
his 'particular province is to go about and preach
the gospel to all, and to strengthen the hands, as
much as in me lies, of every denomination that
preach Jesus Christ in sincerity.' Such being his
views, and remembering also the necessity he is
under to pay frequent visits to this country, it is
not a matter of surprise that he does not organize

societies as Mr. Wesley does. I see that Mr. Wesley's marriage has not at all interfered with his zeal and activity Those who predicted such would be the case should rejoice at their mistake, for his abundant and successful labors prove how poorly a diminution of them could be borne. Fifteen years since Methodism has been founded, and over one hundred itinerant preachers! Societies and chapels in scores of places. What though persecution still exists? Let us recall the declaration so full of meaning, referring to the persecution that followed the stoning of Stephen, that says 'they that were scattered abroad went everywhere preaching the word,' and remember that God can make the 'wrath of man to praise him.' In his own good time he will restrain the 'remainder of wrath,' and when he sees fit make even our 'enemies to be at peace with us.' So I pray that courage and patience may abound with all those to whom 'it is given to suffer' for their Master's sake.

"I thank you for giving me the particulars of my old friend Miss Gilbert's death. I am glad to know her end was so bright and peaceful. It makes heaven nearer to us to realize how easily our loved ones make the exchange of worlds. While we thank God for 'all these his children departed this life in his faith and fear,' let us be careful to follow those who 'through faith and patience inherit the promises.'

"With renewed love from our widening circle to your little band, ever your affectionate

"MOTHER."

→CHAPTER XI.←

LETTER from Mrs. Ethel Lennox to her mother:

"DUDLEY PARSONAGE, SURREY, ENGLAND,
September 15, 1769.

"*My dearest mother:* Prepare for a long letter, as I have much to say to you. In my last communication, you recollect, we were on the eve of taking a journey. My husband needed a holiday. It had been many years since he had enjoyed one, and while we had not finally decided, we inclined somewhat to a visit to the Isle of Wight. Ere our preparations were finally made, however, we heard of the celebration to be observed at Trevecca, in Wales, upon the occasion of the first anniversary of the college for the preparation of clergymen, established there by Lady Huntingdon. We had been interested in this noble charity since its inception. We admire the Christian spirit which governs it, and which admits candidates of any religious opinion, provided they are truly converted to God. They may choose to become clergymen in the Established Church, or in any denomination of Dissenters; it matters not—they are all welcomed. Board, tuition, and a yearly suit of clothes are given each one at the expense of the Countess. We understood there would be a large gathering of the most distinguished evangelists in the country, and we anticipated a rich feast, both mental and spiritual, for you may suppose that we did not hesitate to decide where our vacation should be passed as soon as we were informed of this approaching celebration.

"We both enjoyed the scenery through which we traveled, and what might by some be considered the fatigues of the journey; for, accustomed as we had so long been to a monotonous round of quiet country life, each incident or contrasted experience possessed for us its own peculiar charm of novelty or interest.

"As we approached Trevecca we fell into the company of several who were journeying thither, for, although we were a week in advance of the appointed day, they, like us, anticipated the time, in order to receive all the enjoyment and advantage possible in association of Christians of all shades of religious belief. The scenery became more wild and striking as we drew near, till, as the castle loomed in sight in its romantic and picturesque beauty, we were charmed with the grandeur of the scene. While the ancient building has been rendered not only habitable, but comfortably so, it still sufficiently preserves its air of decay to cause the beholder to appreciate its antique value, and

12

for the mind to rapidly survey the far different scenes its lofty turrets and venerable walls regarded centuries ago. Never did its spacious court-yard witness so goodly a sight, however, as it did for a week before the anniversary, and also for days afterward. A platform was erected from which sermons were delivered to the immense congregations who lingered with spell-bound attention. Exhortations, prayers, and conversions were suitable preparations for the great day of celebration. Early on that morning, the sacrament of the Lord's Supper was administered by Mr. John Wesley and Mr. Shirley—first to a large company of clergymen, then to the students, and afterward to the Countess and her friends, followed by the people. Mr. Wesley preached, and so did Mr. Fletcher, who is the president of the college. In the evening the ancient apostolic 'love-feast' was held, and narratives of Christian experience, songs, and prayers filled the happy hours. The chief charm of the series of meetings, dear mother, was the sweet Christian charity and union which pervaded every spirit. When I stated a few lines back that Messrs. Wesley and Shirley administered the eucharist, did you think that the former is the most prominent exponent of Arminianism in the kingdom, while the latter is equally as pronounced in his adherence to Calvinism? So it is; and how fitting that they should be selected for the holy office! United, and yet divided! Not long since Mr. Wesley wrote: 'When his time is come, God will do what man cannot—namely, make us all of one mind.' To our purblind vision it seems best that that time should be *now*. Our hearts are saddened by the divisions, the controversies—sometimes even degenerating into wrangling—that occasionally have taken place between good men, men truly honest and sincere. We cannot doubt they are so, yet we mourn over their mistaken zeal, their intemperate ardor. O how much better to conduct themselves as in this recent protracted 'love-feast,' it might well be called, at Trevecca, where the comment of every beholder might justly be, 'See how these Christians love one another!'

"I wish here to transcribe for you, as illustrative of the fact that good men can honestly differ, two hymns which have recently appeared—the former by Mr. Charles Wesley, whom you know to be a decided Arminian; the latter by Mr. Toplady, a young itinerant clergyman of Lady Huntingdon's connection of Calvinistic Methodists. In my opinion they are decidedly the two most beautiful hymns that I have ever sent to you. I understand that the authors had had a long and somewhat heated argument upon their peculiar dogmas; but after separating, and before retiring to rest, each, amid the calm and privacy of his own personal devotions, poured out his soul in these transcendent lines. I can fancy, dear mother, the prayers which preceded their composition; the deep regret for having spoken 'unadvisedly with their lips;' the abasement before the Holy One for all their sins of commission and omission; the earnest petition, 'Cleanse thou me from *secret sins;*' and then as the benediction descended from the 'same Jesus' who had so often said, 'Thy sins be forgiven thee,' and with hearts aflame with gratitude and love, they express their emotions in these matchless words. Read them slowly, dear mother, for as you read they will sink into your heart, and find a lasting echo there.

" This is Mr. Wesley's:

> Jesus, lover of my soul,
>   Let me to thy bosom fly,
> While the nearer waters roll,
>   While the tempest still is high:
> Hide me, O my Saviour, hide,
>   Till the storm of life be past;
> Safe into the haven guide,
>   O receive my soul at last!
>
> Other refuge have I none,
>   Hangs my helpless soul on thee:
> Leave, ah! leave me not alone,
>   Still support and comfort me!
> All my trust on thee is stayed,
>   All my help from thee I bring:
> Cover my defenseless head
>   With the shadow of thy wing

Thou, O Christ, art all I want;
  More than all in thee I find:
Raise the fallen, cheer the faint,
  Heal the sick, and lead the blind.
Just and holy is thy name;
  I am all unrighteousness:
False, and full of sin, I am;
  Thou art full of truth and grace.

Plenteous grace with thee is found,
  Grace to cover all my sin:
Let the healing streams abound,
  Make and keep me pure within:
Thou of life the fountain art;
  Freely let me take of thee:
Spring thou up within my heart,
  Rise to all eternity!

And this, Mr. Toplady's:

Rock of ages, cleft for me,
Let me hide myself in thee:
Let the water and the blood,
From thy wounded side which flowed,
Be of sin the double cure,
Save from wrath and make me pure.

Could my tears forever flow,
Could my zeal no languor know,
These for sin could not atone;
Thou must save, and thou alone:
In my hand no price I bring,
Simply to thy cross I cling.

While I draw this fleeting breath,
When my eyes shall close in death,

> When I rise to worlds unknown,
> And behold thee on thy throne,
> Rock of ages, cleft for me,
> Let me hide myself in thee.

Now, compare them, dear mother, and observe how utterly absent all diverse opinions; how completely merged into one full, flowing stream of love are the small rills of sect or party; how the need, the desire of one Lord, one faith, one baptism is preëminent. 'Jesus, lover of my soul!' Ah! there it is—the blessed gospel! Can mortal tongue frame sweeter words? How our inmost being sinks to rest upon the precious assurance that *Jesus* is the 'lover of *my* soul!' Then,

> Hide me, O my Saviour, hide,
> Till the storm of life be past.

Now, mark the surprising identity of thought, almost of expression:

> Rock of ages, cleft for me,
> Let me hide myself in thee.

Again:

> Let the water and the blood,
> From thy wounded side which flowed,
> Be of sin the double cure,
> *Save from wrath and make me pure.*

Compare:

> Let the healing streams abound,
> *Make* and *keep me pure* within.

Once more:

> Thou must save, and thou alone.

> Thou, O Christ, art all I want!

Only read:

> In my hand no price I bring,
> Simply to thy cross I cling.

> Other refuge have I none,
> Hangs my helpless soul on thee.

Finally:

> While I draw this fleeting breath,
> When my eyes shall close in death.

> Safe into the haven guide,
> O receive my soul at last!

"Observe that the meter is the same, so that one tune can be used for both, and the words interchange so naturally that it is pleasant to rearrange them as I did a moment ago. Both these ministers are devoting their lives to the service of God, and doubtless regard the composition of these hymns as a very little thing—a mere audible, casual utterance of a feeling of love and trust with which they are familiar; but to my mind it appears that if they had lived lives of seclusion, unknowing and unknown to the busy throng of men except by these two isolated hymns, like the wondrous century plant blooming but once in its life-time, they would still have done a blessed work which will far outlast their own brief lives.

"My husband and I were glad of the opportunity afforded by our visit to Trevecca to become acquainted with Lady Huntingdon, her chaplains, and other evangelists with whose names we had long been familiar—Romaine, Madan, Venn, and others. I must relate to you a beautiful answer the latter made when asked if a young minister, whose name had been mentioned, was a Calvinist or an Arminian. 'I really do not know,' he said; 'he is a sincere disciple of the Lord Jesus Christ, and that is of infinitely more importance than his being a disciple of Calvin or Arminius.'

"Lady Huntingdon is certainly a wonderful woman. She spends her fortune to the uttermost—even her jewels are thrown into the treasury of the Lord. The sermons preached in her parlors reach a class of hearers that would not otherwise hear the stirring appeals. And yet, if I could, I should rather be with her when, accompanied by her chaplains, she travels from county to county, and thousands hear and believe the glad tidings. I wish I could have been at Cheltenham when Whitefield—denied admittance to the church—preached, as Wesley had done, in the church-yard, a tombstone his pulpit, his text 'Ho! every one that thirsteth, come ye to the waters,' and an immense assembly thrilled by his eloquence. It were worth the journey there, methinks, to see those weary and heavy-laden ones listening to the urgent embassador, and accepting the call to come unto Him who would give rest to their souls. How could any resist the persuasive tones and matchless eloquence of that loving spirit? When so oppressed with his message and with solicitude for the unconverted around, words failed him and a flood of tears proved the yearning of his heart, how could any fail to recognize in him the 'mind that was in Jesus'—who wept in compassion over the ones who disregarded his tender mercy—and not yield to their Saviour's love?

"It was a Pentecostal time, and many were converted. This gives you an idea of the excursions taken by this devoted lady and her ardent band, every one of whom is eminently successful in doing good. Chapels are established by her aid in England, Wales, and Ireland. She has mapped England into six districts or circuits, and sent out itinerants to preach everywhere in places large or small which are not already similarly occupied.

"The great activity shown by the preachers in her religious 'connection,' combined with Mr. Wesley's unwearied zeal and ceaseless journeyings, which are imitated by his followers, has revived evangelical religion in every portion of the kingdom. Although persecution by tongue and pen in high places and by ignorant mobs has not altogether ceased, it has diminished, and a broader field and a firmer foothold have been gained steadily year

after year.   Mr. Wesley's active labors would indicate no time or inclination for literary work, while
on the other hand, viewing the immense aggregate
of his voluminous and varied writings, one might
suppose his life was altogether that of a scribe.

"In returning from Trevecca, we tarried a few
days in London, paying a short visit to Uncle George,
who was at his city house.   There, one day at din-
ner, we met Dr. Benjamin Franklin, the agent rep-
resenting your province in Great Britain.   Apart
from the fact that so large a portion of my family
reside in Georgia, I feel great interest in its welfare.
When, in 1763, land southward to the St. Mary's
River was annexed to it, I felt a thrill of pleasure,
for I knew how much more prosperous she would
become, and how much more safely her population
would dwell within her borders, because of the cessation of Spanish rule and French intrigue in that
direction.   The knowledge that King George's dominions extended to the Gulf of Mexico must have
given every inhabitant a pleasurable feeling of security.

"The conversation at Uncle George's dinner-
table was naturally directed to the condition of the
colonies.   The passage of the Stamp Act in 1765,
the great excitement and opposition to it in America during its existence, and the rejoicing when it
was repealed the following year, were all dwelt
upon at length.

"Uncle George—who, you well know, has always been one of Pitt's warmest adherents—grew eloquent over the scene in Parliament the night, or rather the early dawn, when the final vote was taken. Lord Chatham, regardless of his painful infirmities, walked into the House on crutches, and claiming justice for English subjects who had loyally supported their mother-country through three wars, demanded for them the repeal of the act— rewarded for his humanity and self-denial when a large majority voted in favor of justice and liberty. Uncle George's face glowed with pleasure as he described the shouts of triumph that then ascended, and also when he alluded to the acknowledgment by grateful America of Pitt's services in her behalf.

"Dr. Franklin gave us a vivid description of the extent of the opposition to the unjust enactment as illustrated in connection with your own city—of course it is familiar to you, but we had never heard it before. He told us how, in a pressing emergency, near seventy vessels which were in the port of Savannah used stamps in being cleared, fearing to depart without them. Under the circumstances the citizens consented to the use of stamps for the first and only time. South Carolina was violently offended at their action, resolving that no provisions should be shipped to Georgia, and that every vessel trading there should be burned. These intemperate and unneighborly threats were absolutely carried into execution. Two vessels that had cleared for Savannah were captured before they crossed Charleston bar, and were totally destroyed with their cargoes.

"What a tremendous state of excitement does this indicate! It makes me tremble for the future, for many think the question is not permanently settled. The opposition is determined. The king regrets the repeal. Lord Chatham's health forces him to lead the life of a recluse. Fox and Burke throw all their eloquence and influence upon the side with which we sympathize, but Townshend's policy of coercion may yet prevail. Dr. Franklin resolutely declared that he 'would freely spend nineteen shillings in the pound to defend his right of giving or refusing the other shilling,' at the same time asserting that the vast majority of the colonists were in perfect accord with his views, so large a majority that the whole of America might be considered as virtually a unit. Have you omitted referring to this subject in your letters, dear mother, for fear of causing me uneasiness? In our quiet hamlet, I admit, it has attracted my attention very slightly; but now my ears are opened, and I hear the distant rumbling which may precede a frightful storm. God forbid! Our case is but one of a thousand. How many there are who have loved ones on both sides of the mighty ocean! and how many pulses are quickening with apprehensions of

a vague terror they are unwilling to put into words!
But 'sufficient unto the day is the evil thereof.' I
will not go forth to meet a trouble that may never
reach me.

"My boys are at Oxford, great students, but
active, athletic fellows, improving both brain and
brawn. Far better still, they are Christians, and
practical in their endeavors to do good. My Eva
is growing steadily into lovely womanhood, and my
younger children are docile, intelligent, and affectionate. Mrs. Susanna Wesley, who won my admiration when I was a girl, has been my model
since I became a mother. I remember her uniform
faithfulness to each child, and endeavor to imitate
it. Recollecting the vital importance of recogniz-
ing the individuality of each young immortal committed to my maternal guidance, I do my best, and
leave results with God, praying him to 'establish
the work of my hands.'

"Your loving daughter, ETHEL LENNOX."

⇢ CHAPTER XII. ⇠

LETTER from Mrs. Woodville to her daughter,
Mrs. Lennox:

"SAVANNAH, IN GEORGIA, Aug. 11, 1776.

"*My dear daughter:* I will write this letter, although I fear it will never reach you. In these

troublous times, when we are more than ever anxious for rapid and direct communication with each
other, the delay and suspense connected with our
correspondence are hard to bear. Still, we must
continue our efforts, and if occasionally one of our
many letters reaches its destination, our gratification will be proportionate to its rarity. I hope this
package will reach you promptly, though probably
the great news it contains will not be news to you
when you have read it. The intelligence of the
event which I now relate to you only reached us
yesterday, although it took place over one month
ago. It is no less than a declaration of independence on the part of the thirteen British colonies,
by which they throw off allegiance to King George
of England, and assert that they are free and sovereign States. They have assumed the title of the
United States of America, and have bound themselves together for mutual defense and protection,
under certain limitations and conditions. On the
fourth day of July last past, in Independence Hall,
Philadelphia, in the State—I must now say—of
Pennsylvania, the Declaration of Independence,
drawn up by Thomas Jefferson, of Virginia, was
signed by representatives from every State. Those
from Georgia were Messrs. Lyman Hall, George
Walton, and Button Gwinnett. A copy of this
document was delivered yesterday by an express
messenger into the hands of our president—Bulloch

—and was read aloud four times in as many places in the city. First, our Provincial Council was at once assembled, and listened with admiration and approbation to its contents. Then they adjourned to the public square, where, amidst the loudly expressed enthusiasm of the assembled citizens, it was again read. Then a procession was formed of the officials, soldiery, and militia, and marching to the liberty pole, for the third time it was listened to. Thirteen volleys from cannon and small arms succeeded. After the fourth and last reading at the battery at the trustees' garden, a salute was fired from the siege guns. A vast concourse went from place to place, and rent the air with acclamations. At night the town was illuminated, and King George Third was buried in effigy in front of the court-house. An immense funeral procession was formed, composed apparently of every citizen and soldier in the neighborhood. The slow-beating drums were muffled, and so much form and circumstance observed that the mock obsequies were truly impressive. Doubtless similar demonstrations have been made everywhere. As we were farthest removed from Philadelphia, so were we the last to receive the tidings. Now we may look for a protracted war, and the God of battles only knows the result. We talk of our righteous cause, and are resolved to win the fight; but other causes as good as ours have been blotted out forever in blood and darkness; and England's power is great, and we are few and feeble. But I suppose my forebodings are due, to a great extent, to my age. I was seventy-two last birthday, you know, my dear; but then your father, so hale and hearty in his eightieth year, is as great a rebel as Annie's youngest little curly pate. Certainly there are no stronger rebels than my sons and grandsons. Do you remember how Edward and Arthur in their childhood rejected all King George's claims, and declared themselves subjects of our good Gen. Oglethorpe? That feeling has grown with their growth and strengthened with their strength. Their children have imbibed it, and each registered himself as a 'Son of Liberty' in the first inauguration of that band. Yes, they are all engaged in the service of their country, and have taken an active part in every demonstration that has been made. Early in the year a battalion consisting of eight companies was raised, and every Woodville able to bear arms was enrolled at once. Habersham and Whitefield are at the seat of war. They were both as eager for the fray as young war-horses. The first overt act of our excited citizens was to break into the powder-magazine about a year ago and abstract and secrete about six hundred pounds. In vain did Gov. Wright offer rewards for the apprehension of the offenders. Public sympathy was too strongly in their favor for any revelation to be

made.   About two months afterward the first capture by order of any Congress in America was
made, and by a Georgia schooner, the first provincial vessel commissioned for naval warfare. The
forces of Carolina and Georgia had united to effect
the capture, which was of a British ship containing
a large supply of powder for the use of the Royalists and Indians.   The share of our men was nine
thousand pounds.   Over half of this was sent to
Philadelphia, to be used where it was so much needed.

"While witnessing the intense, enthusiastic excitement of yesterday, a spectator might have thought
that the charge which has been brought against our
colony of reluctance to join her sisters in their
efforts for freedom was utterly groundless.   Indeed,
all hesitancy has vanished now.   The first gun
fired at Lexington was the signal for union of
methods as well as aims and desires.   Truth com-
pels me to say, however, that I can readily see why
some should hesitate.   We had fewer causes of
grievance than any other colony, fewer wrongs to
redress, perhaps more favors to acknowledge; but
when force was added to fraud—when England
reached forth murderous hands to the children who
resisted spoliation and, acting from the principles
she herself had taught, would not submit to taxa-
tion without representation—the past was forgotten,
and self-respect and self-protection prompted resist-
ance—ay, even to the death.

13

"I find that I am writing in a very patriotic
way—from my stand-point. I can hardly expect
to find a like ardor in your circle, though I am
sure of your intense sympathy. As a colony, we
found it difficult too to act directly in opposition to
our loyal, firm, unbending Governor. No royal
governor in America has possessed in a higher degree the qualities to win the love and respect of
his people, or to deserve the confidence and approbation of his king. There was but one thing left
for our 'Sons of Liberty' to do, which was effected
with considerable respect but firm resolve. Maj.
Joseph Habersham quietly arrested him in his own
residence. Gov. Wright submitted with calmness,
but in two or three weeks, wearied with seclusion,
he effected his escape from the rear of his dwelling, and reaching the river he first got safely to
Bonaventure and finally to a British ship lying in
the mouth of the river.

"Now we are a free and independent State.
Shall a royal governor ever again represent a foreign power? Could we look into the future for a
short space — say even one decade—would our
eyes behold the English colors again floating over
us? or would an unknown flag, at present not devised, show that victory had been ours? Alas!
my heart grows sick at the thought of the precious
blood that will flow in either event. O when will
swords be beaten into plowshares, and spears into

pruning-hooks, and the sound of war be heard no more forever?

"Last week I drove out to Bethesda. I wished once more, before my strength failed me, to see the spot where the sainted Mr. Whitefield had so earnestly desired should be established a college for the education of Southern youth. How he labored for this end, and for the orphanage which was the object of his loving and unceasing self-denial! He crossed the ocean thirteen times. He preached thousands of sermons, and collected moneys with all his energies. When Gov. Wright laid the corner-stone of the college he hoped would be a permanent and flourishing institution, how encouraged was the good man to whom we all owed so much! But his race was well-nigh run. His health had been failing for years. He was worn and weary, as he said so pathetically just as he had finished that two hours' sermon the very day before he died: 'Lord Jesus, I am weary *in* thy work, but not *of* thy work.' Most fitting and deserved were the marks of respect shown to him in this town. Every yard of black cloth was bought to drape churches and State-house. Flags were at half-mast. Governor and council, dressed in mourning, went in procession to hear a funeral-sermon. It must have been touching to hear the funeral discourse Mr. John Wesley delivered in the Tabernacle near Moorfields, and to remember that these almost life-long friends had agreed that the survivor should preach the funeral-sermon of the one who first had died. His description of his friend's chief characteristics was accurate and just—'unparalleled zeal, indefatigable activity, tender-heartedness to the afflicted, and charitableness toward the poor, nice and unblemished modesty, the most generous friendship, frankness and openness of conversation, unflinching courage, and steadiness in whatever he undertook for his Master's sake.' These clauses in the sermon, though, most touched my heart: 'How few have we known of so kind a temper, of such large and flowing affections! Was it not principally by this that the hearts of others were so strangely drawn and knit to him? Can any thing but love beget love? This shone in his very countenance, and breathed in all his words, whether in public or private. Was it not this which, quick and penetrating as lightning, flew from heart to heart? which gave that life to his sermons, his conversations, his letters? Ye are witnesses.' And truly we are, and testify of the wonderful power of this apostle of love. Was it not remarkable that so soon after his death his beloved Bethesda should be laid in ashes? How irresistible the feeling of satisfaction at the thought that he was spared that sorrow! He bequeathed it, as you know, to Lady Huntingdon, together with other property connected with it. She rebuilt, out of her private means, a smaller house to serve the few pupils that were left. When her missionary band came over and preached so successfully, not only here but extensively through the country, she must have greatly rejoiced. What a saint she is! What vast good she has accomplished! If no other labors could send her blessed name down to an admiring posterity, this single enterprise was sufficient. To organize and equip a band of missionaries to cross the ocean and impart a portion of their ardent zeal to the feeble and languishing churches here; to seek after the salvation of Indians and Africans, as well as those whose disregard of sacred subjects was not attributable to their ignorance, but to their hardness of heart; to labor so unweariedly that singular success crowned their efforts, was a work the magnitude of which was sufficient to have laded her memory with love and honor.

"But this undertaking is only an episode in her busy and fruitful life. Other preaching excursions, more royal than any 'kingly progress' Britain has ever seen, are frequent incidents in her experience: sixty-four chapels which she has greatly helped to build; one hundred thousand pounds which she has given to further the cause of religion; the imagined demands of rank and state; the pride of life in residence, adornment, and service—all yielding their claims, all being relinquished and counted as naught for the sake of the spiritual needs of her fellow-creatures. I have sometimes thought with what intense earnestness she has asked the question, 'Lord, what wilt thou have ME to do?' Clearly has she heard the answer, and in response has been given her all—time, influence, money, ease, soul, body, heart, and strength.

"How wonderful it is that in one generation two such leading spirits should appear as Lady Huntingdon and Mr. John Wesley! So similar, so identical in many respects—in their love, zeal, self-denial; in their strength of character, and in executive ability—while they honestly differ in some points of religious belief. Thank God, both can say, 'Grace be with all them that love our Lord Jesus Christ in sincerity.' That is the test for earth and heaven, and we need seek for no other. What could be more expressive of Christian unity and love than Mr. Whitefield's letter to Mr. Wesley some years ago? 'I thank you, dear sir, for praying for me. I have been upon my knees praying for you and yours, and that nothing but love and lowliness and simplicity may be among us. For Christ's sake let us not be divided among ourselves.'

"If this spirit were but universal with all who love Christ, how rapidly would his dominion extend over the earth, and harsh judgments and heated controversies be unknown forever! This quotation I make from one of Mr. Wesley's pamphlets is very appropriate, I think, to this subject. He writes: 'Let us bear with one another, remembering it is the prerogative of the great God to pierce through all his own infinite schemes with an unerring eye, to surround them with an all-comprehensive view, to grasp them all in one single survey, and to spread a reconciling light over all their immense varieties. Man must yet grapple with difficulties in this dusky twilight, but God, in his time, will irradiate the earth more plentifully with his light and truth.' We can await his good pleasure in this matter as in all others—can we not, my child? To you it may be granted to see that blessed time when 'righteousness shall cover the earth as the waters cover the sea'—but for me, I doubt not my joy is nearer. Though blessed with a vigorous old age, yet I feel that my life is near its close. I do not write this to sadden you, dear child—why should it? I rejoice to be able to say when I at last become 'absent from the body, I shall be present with the Lord;' therefore, if I precede you to the home whither we are tending, I charge you not to grieve, but rather—as Susanna Wesley directed her children standing around the bed from which her happy spirit was soon to wing its flight—'when I am released, sing a song of praise to God.'

"In writing this to you I feel somewhat as shipwrecked mariners may, when recounting their experience they place the manuscript in a bottle and commit it to the waves, not knowing whether human eye will ever trace the lines, or whether they shall be finally ingulfed in the deep waters; so I write, knowing the probabilities that this may never reach you, yet feeling that every month increases them. Therefore, my beloved daughter, I am inclined to speak as I have done, and to commit you and yours into the care of our loving Heavenly Father. He, and he alone, knows what the future has in store for us; he, and he alone, can prepare us for it. With unwavering confidence in his wisdom and kindness, whether battles rage or the calm of peace surrounds us, whether we sit beside one fireside or oceans roll between us, for life or death, for time or eternity, I yield myself and each of our dear ones to his care, praying that in that day when he numbereth his jewels not one may be absent.

"Your loving   MOTHER."

➻CHAPTER XIII.↢

THE tide of War was rising upon the new nation of the New World. When it should reach its highest mark, ah! who could tell? When would the sword be sheathed? when the flow of blood be stayed? When would sweet Peace once more turn her long-averted, affrighted face and smile in gladness upon the land which had so yearned for her presence?

Georgia was not at first the seat of war; the horrors of Brandywine, Germantown, and Monmouth were spared her, and the atrocities and butchery of Wyoming were unknown. Finally hostile demonstrations from Florida broke the monotony of dread and suspense, but, although the torch almost destroyed the village of Midway, and slaves, cattle, and property were stolen, the object of the raid—an attack on Savannah—was unaccomplished. However, in November of the same year—1778—two thousand British troops from New York were too formidable for the few militia and six hundred American regulars. In addition to their superior numbers, treachery was employed to guide the enemy to a position of attack from the rear. Thus encompassed, defeat was assured, and Savannah fell into the hands of the British. At the same time the shipping was captured and all communication with South Carolina cut off. These advantages being promptly followed up, in a short time Georgia was entirely in the hands of the Royal power, one post after another being secured until finally even Augusta was lost to the State.

Many of the citizens, however, placing their wives and children in safety in South Carolina, returned to the Savannah River, and a border warfare, as it were, was continued for some months. Finally a successful engagement or two supplied these brave patriots with about six hundred horses and a large quantity of arms, equipments, and clothing, as valuable as the enkindled hope and restored confidence that encouraged them still to battle against such almost hopeless odds. One success assured another, their swelling numbers attracted more, until the Tories were routed from Upper Georgia, and Col. Campbell—the British officer in command—determined to evacuate Augusta, which he did speedily, leaving behind him military stores of much value.

As this city had been designated by the executive council as the seat of government when Savannah was captured, as soon as the enemy retired a called meeting was held—in July, 1779—and means devised to establish at least a form of government loyal to the compact of the new confederation. In the meantime, Gov. Wright had been reinstated in Savannah, and the once quiet colony of Georgia was the theater of two opposing governments, in both of which were violent opposers and ardent adherents; in both were zealous workers for the cause they espoused; in both was the commonwealth in a wretched condition, torn, distracted, and impoverished.

There was a day not long before when hope revived and the independence of the united colonies was regarded as beyond doubt, when the King of France was proclaimed the "Protector of the rights of mankind," for treaties of commerce and alliance had been ratified between Louis XVI. and the Continental Congress. But this event was not rejoiced over in Georgia as it had been in her sister States. They, it is true, had heard more of the cannon's roar. The "pomp and circumstance," the agony and groans of cruel war had been theirs, and now, louder and higher than all else, they heard and saw the promise of future deliverance. But, alas! our poor State, bowed beneath the calamities of internecine strife, found her ears too heavy, her eyes too dim, her heart too sorrowful to look up and receive the hope that inspired her sisters.

At last the night of her despondency seemed about to approach its close, for unexpectedly within the river, that had so long been familiar with vessels of the foe, appeared the French fleet—twenty ships of the line, ten frigates, and a cutter. Capturing several English vessels they ascended the Savannah River, and every appearance indicated that the town would soon be released from the grasp of Royalty. It is needless to trace the cause and reasons of the unfortunate delays, of the lost opportunities. The golden moment passed by, and poor Savannah—disappointed in all her expectations, after the weary siege was ended, after the disastrous attack was over, after streams of blood had flowed in vain from her most gallant and patriotic sons—fell back, despairingly, into the clutch of her enemy, having by her efforts to free herself but tightened his grasp and aroused renewed activity of malice.

Of the fallen braves history yet speaks. Perpetuated in street, in square, in public buildings, in monumental marble, is the name of the gallant Pole who, having failed to secure liberty to the land of his birth, gave his sword and his life to a weak and struggling infant nation. Never will Georgia forget Pulaski while history is remembered and valor and gratitude exist. Noble he was by birth and nature; but not less brave or patriotic was the modest, intrepid Jasper, refusing any title higher than that of sergeant, yet giving his life gladly to protect the colors placed in his charge because of his devoted courage. In his dying-moments he sent the sword presented to him by Gov. Rutledge, of South Carolina, because of his services in the defense of Fort Moultrie, saying: "Give it to my father, and tell him I have worn it with honor; if he should weep, say to him his son died in the hope of a better life." Georgia keeps his memory green. Little did he think, as his breath grew shorter and more faint, that his name should be spoken daily in a ward of the city he died in the effort to liberate, never dreaming of the growth, the prosperity it should achieve; that a county in his native State should be honored by being called for him; that a military company of volunteers should inscribe his name upon their flag,

and proudly march beneath its shadow, having followed it to victory on many a battle-field, even on
a foreign soil; that a century afterward his gallant
deeds should be recounted to admiring thousands,
when, during a celebration held in honor of him,
the foundation-stone of a monument to his memory
would be laid, amid enthusiastic demonstrations.

A day of public thanksgiving was appointed by
the Royalists, but little did the patriots sympathize
with them—impoverished, oppressed, and discouraged, hope for a season seemed to have bid their
world farewell.

The battles of Cowpens and Guilford, however,
which took place early in 1781, revived the sinking
courage of the Georgians, although these victories
did not take place within the limits of their State.
The successful siege of Augusta inspired fresh hope,
so that the surrender of Lord Cornwallis in October of the same year was hailed by them as joyfully as by the other colonies. When the gallant
Gen. Wayne entered the State in the following year
with orders to "reïnstate, as far as might be possible,
the authority of the Union within the limits of
Georgia," and with his wisdom, tact, and activity
succeeded in wresting from the enemy all the country except Savannah, we may readily suppose that
it needed but the order from Sir Guy Carleton that
that town should be evacuated to impart enthusiasm and confidence of speedy and permanent lib-

eration to the hitherto dejected and downtrodden inhabitants. Soon after, the British troops retired, and Gen. Wayne took possession.

Happy in present peace, and hopeful for the future, the people went to work heartily to build up the waste places—to restore, to improve, to establish their homes once more. In January, 1783, they elected Dr. Lyman Hall as Governor; and when the treaty of peace, in which Great Britain acknowledged the independence of the United States, was signed at Paris the following September, Georgia, in company with her sister States, turned her back upon the past, forgot all former disasters, sufferings, and privations, and in her place, a component part of a young nation, started on a career of prosperity, of growth, of freedom such as the world has never seen paralleled. The tiny, feeble colony planted by Oglethorpe on the bluff of Yamacraw was now a free and sovereign State. How must the heart of its noble founder have swelled with pride as he contemplated the flourishing tree grown from the seed he had sown! He was then in a vigorous old age, still admired and respected by all. His distinguishing characteristics had been *wisdom, justice,* and *moderation*—never more demonstrated than during his life and labors in Georgia. How wonderfully appropriate, then, that these words, descriptive of his peculiar traits, should be inscribed on the seal and coat-of-arms of this great Commonwealth—an aspiration, an exhortation for all her earnest sons!

Gen. Oglethorpe died in 1785. Quoting the words of an eloquent living author *: "Edmund Burke regarded him as the most extraordinary person of whom he had ever read, because he had founded a province and lived to see it severed from the empire which created it, and erected into an independent State. A short time before his death he paid his respects to Mr. John Adams, who had arrived in London as the first minister plenipotentiary of the United States of America to the Court of St. James. There was something peculiarly interesting in this interview. He who had planted Georgia and nurtured it during the earliest stages of its dependent condition as a colony held converse with him who had come to a royal court as the representative of its separate national existence. His body reposes within Cranham Church. A memorial tablet there proclaims his excellences; but here the Savannah repeats to the Altamaha the story of his virtues and of his valor, and the Atlantic publishes to the mountains the greatness of his fame, for all Georgia is his living, speaking monument."

* Col. C. C. Jones's History of Georgia.

→CHAPTER XIV.←

WHILE the political life of Georgia had been revolutionized amidst years of strife and bloodshed, so that loyalty to the King of England had become a thing of the past, adherence—blind, unreasoning adherence—to the Church of England, in defiance of expediency and the promptings of religion and common sense, was also trembling to its fall.

Mr. Wesley—a High-churchman by birth, education, taste, and the powerful force of habit—was extremely reluctant for the societies he had formed ever to separate from the Episcopal Church, the Established Church of the realm. He fondly hoped that as united societies they would work within its limits, no matter how numerous they should ever become.

Any one whose interest is aroused on this subject can obtain various books which will give information both full and satisfactory to the impartial reader.

For the purpose of this sketch it is sufficient to notice the surprising coincidence in point of time that made 1784, the year following that in which the independence of the United States of America was acknowledged by Great Britain, the very date when in England the deed of declaration was executed, and when in America the first formal organization of Methodism was effected. Well might this be called the "grand climacteric year of Methodism." The object of the deed referred to—which has been called Methodism's *Magna Charta*—was to explain the words "yearly conference of the people called Methodists," and to declare what persons are members of the said conference, and how the succession and identity thereof are to be continued; or, in other words, to form the Methodist societies into a legally incorporated institution. A few days afterward it was enrolled in the high court of chancery; and although the effects of it were gradual, and the knowledge of "whereunto it might grow" was at that time indeed limited, still a departure from exact parallel lines was then made, the divergence growing steadily wider until the present position of independence and disconnection has been reached.

The organization of the Methodist Episcopal Church of America was not only the outgrowth of a necessity formed by the demands of both preachers and people—a necessity which could be supplied in no other way—but the result of a conviction Mr. Wesley had felt for over forty years, and which had not been acted upon because he felt the time for it had not yet come, and because he earnestly hoped it would never arrive. When, however, the Revolutionary War had not only severed old relations with the king, but also the Church of England; when eighty-one itinerant, some hun-

14

dreds of local American preachers, and fifteen thousand members combined to demand the administration of the sacraments which had been denied them for many years; when the English bishops declined to go or send to their relief—then at last Mr. Wesley felt that it was time to act upon his convictions. These were, that the distinction between bishops and preachers was one of *order* rather than of *office;* also that although "episcopal ordination was expedient, it was not absolutely necessary." These being his long-established opinions, it is not surprising that he should also assert: "I firmly believe I am a scriptural *episcopos* as much as any man in England, for the uninterrupted succession I know to be a fable, which no man ever did or can prove." *

The reasonable consequence of such deep-rooted convictions coming into collision with old prejudices would naturally be the yielding up of the latter, especially when to adhere to them would be to act contrary to the immense pressure brought to bear against them and in favor of an extension of the special doctrines and mode of worship to which he had consecrated his life. And so it came to pass that Dr. Thomas Coke was ordained by Wesley, who was assisted by other ordained ministers, as a superintendent or bishop to go to America and unite Francis Asbury with him in his superin-

---

* Tyerman's Life of Wesley.

tendency by ordaining him also to the great work.
Mr. Asbury desired the concurrence of his fellow-
preachers in this action, which was heartily given;
and in Baltimore, at the Christmas Conference,
December 24, 1784, Dr. Coke, assisted by the German Bishop Otterbein, ordained Francis Asbury,
and he and Dr. Coke were elected, or indorsed—by
sixty traveling preachers who were present—as su-
perintendents, or bishops, of the Methodist Episcopal Church in America.

Thus we see Baltimore the cradle of American
Methodism, as Philadelphia was the cradle of American independence. One State after another experienced the benefits of the latter; so also grew the
influence and blessings of the former. In three or
four years organized Methodism was extended into
Georgia, and Bishop Asbury had in that State a
band of vigorous, devoted, apostolic men who, regardless of dangers, fatigue, and privations, were
willing to give their lives to win souls to God.
Among that band are names sweet to the ears of
true Methodists to this day.

It would seem as if the two great acts accomplished in the year 1784, when Mr. Wesley was
eighty-one years of age, would have been a suitable
conclusion to his life of labor, and that in his extreme old age he might have said, "Let thy servant depart in peace, for mine eyes have seen thy
salvation," and that the remainder of his days

would have been passed in quiet and repose. But such was not the case or his desire, for like Moses, the great lawgiver—who had also led a great people to the promised land, though the weight of four-score years rested upon him—it might be said "his eye was not dim, nor his natural force abated." He wrote: "To-day I entered on my eighty-second year, and found myself just as strong to labor, and as fit for any exercise of body or mind, as I was forty years ago. I do not impute this to second causes, but to the sovereign Lord of all. It is he who bids the sun of life stand still so long as it pleaseth him. I am as strong at eighty-one as I was at twenty-one, but abundantly more healthy." The next year he wrote: "It is eleven years since I have felt any such thing as weariness; many times I speak till my voice fails, and I can speak no longer; frequently I walk till my strength fails, and I can walk no farther; yet even then I feel no sensation of weariness, but am perfectly easy from head to foot." A greater cause of rejoicing, however, he found in the increasing prosperity of the work of God. He says: "I have now gone through every province and visited all the chief societies, and I have found far the greater part of them increasing both in number and strength." Then, in alluding to himself, he adds: "I am become, I know not how, an honorable man. The scandal of the cross is ceased, and all the kingdom, rich and poor, papists and Protestants, behave with courtesy and seeming good-will. It seems as if I had well-nigh finished my course, and our Lord was giving me an honorable discharge." But if so, the discharge was a season of prolonged activity. His incessant journeying and frequent preaching ceased for a few months, while he devoted himself to the writing of Mr. Fletcher's life, steadily applying himself from five o'clock in the morning to eight o'clock at night. "I can write no longer than fifteen hours a day," he remarked, "without hurting my eyes." After this literary labor, returning to his active life, and while eighty-five years old, he preached in the space of eight weeks more than eighty sermons in fifty-seven different towns and villages.

And so, unwearied, he went down to the "narrow stream," which was but a shallow rill for his crossing. Seven days before his death he preached eighteen miles from his home in London, having risen at his usual hour—four o'clock. Returning to City Road, he was compelled to yield to weakness. Fever supervened, and on March 2, 1791, aged almost eighty-eight years, he calmly yet triumphantly fell asleep in Jesus and awoke to everlasting life. His most remarkable utterances upon his death-bed were: "I the chief of sinners am, but Jesus died for me;" "The best of all is, God is with us;" "He giveth his servants rest;" "The

Lord of hosts is with us; the God of Jacob is our refuge." And so, after a long and useful life, passed away from earth this remarkable, this wonderful man—the founder of Methodism.

Of him it may be said with emphasis, "He builded wiser than he knew." It is true "he originated no new principles, but continued and emphasized old ones; he discovered no new truths, but rescued and stressed old ones that had gone out of fashion; he created no new moral forces, but following providential openings took advantage of those that had been unused, or misused, or disused."* So, even while inaugurating the grand ecclesiastical system that holds his name in special reverence, he acted, as it were, under protest of compelling circumstances. Shall we not believe that he was led by a way he knew not? Like other great and good men who preceded him, his fame increases, and posterity admire and revere him more than did his own generation. "He rests from his labors, and his works do follow him," greater, more universally diffused than he had ever pictured.

It is but natural to turn with interest to the two men so prominent in the early history of American Methodism, Bishops Coke and Asbury. Thomas Coke, the "Foreign Minister of Methodism," crossed the Atlantic eighteen times at his own charges, in pursuit of his great desire to do good to men, prov-

* Bishop McTyeire.

ing the sincerity of his exclamation: "O that I had the voice of a trumpet and the wing of an angel, that I might fly north, south, east, and west to proclaim the gospel of Christ!" In addition to missionary work in Nova Scotia, West Indies, Gibraltar, Sierra Leone, and the superintendency of the missions on the American continent, as well as the presidency of the British and Irish Conferences, his interest was aroused in behalf of India. With difficulty he obtained permission to go to Ceylon and Java. At first the Conference denied his request, but when he urged his petition with the eloquence of tears, and declared his determination to defray the expenses of himself and six comrades, brother missionaries, out of his private purse, they could no longer refuse. He was in his sixty-seventh year, but his zeal knew no bounds of age or time—he did not live to reach his place of destination. A stroke of apoplexy in mid ocean ended his useful career. His body was committed to the coral depths of the Pacific Ocean, his soul went to the reward that awaits those who, like their Divine Master, spend their lives in "going about doing good."

As the "blood of the martyrs is the seed of the Church," so the death of enthusiasts often results in a fresh impetus to the cause for which they labored; so in this case Mr. Richard Watson said: "The work in which Dr. Coke's soul had so greatly de-

lighted, and in the prosecution of which he died,
seemed to derive new interest from those retrospec-
tions to which the contemplation of his life, character, and labors necessarily led; and his loss, while
it dictated the necessity of the exertions of the
many to supply the efforts of one, diffused the spirit
of holy zeal with those regrets which consecrated
his memory." Missionary societies were formed and
great interest in the cause was aroused. Larger
contributions of money and more extensive plans
for the conversion of the heathen were inaugurated,
so that never since the days of the apostles had the
cause of missions created such wide-spread notice
or taken on such a vigorous growth. Let the name
of this devoted missionary be ever cherished, as it
richly deserves.

Now, turning to view his colleague, we find the
most complete synopsis of the life and labors of
Bishop Francis Asbury—the only one of Mr. Wesley's English itinerants who remained in America
during the Revolutionary War—is given by Mr.
Tyerman, in his "Life of John Wesley." He says:

"The son of peasant parents, Asbury began to
preach in Staffordshire, while yet a boy seventeen
years of age, and in 1771 came to Bristol to embark
for America without a single penny in his pocket.
His first text in America was in perfect harmony
with the forty-five years he spent in wandering
through its woods and prairies: 'I determined not

to know any thing among you, save Jesus Christ and him crucified.' As early as 1776 he made it a rule, besides traveling and preaching, to read one hundred pages daily, and to spend three hours out of every twenty-four in private prayer. Cabins of the most miserable description were in thousands of instances his happy homes; and often when his horse cast a shoe in the wide wilderness, in the absence of a blacksmith's shop this grand old Bishop of the American Methodists would make a piece of a bull's hide bound about his horse's foot serve in the place of iron. His daily rides were often from thirty to fifty miles, over mountains and swamps, through bridgeless rivers and pathless woods, his horse frequently weary and lame, and he himself wet, cold, and hungry. For forty-five years, when steam-boats, stage-coaches, railways, and almost roads were utterly unknown, Asbury made a tour of the American States, traveling never less than five thousand, and often more than six thousand, miles a year, and this generally on horseback; climbing mountains; creeping down declivities; winding along valleys whose only inhabitants were birds, wild beasts, and Indians; crossing extended prairies without a companion and without a guide; fording foaming rivers; wading through the most dangerous swamps, where one false step might have ingulfed him in a boggy grave. Usually he preached at least once every week-day and thrice on Sunday, during his ministry in America delivering more than twenty thousand sermons. His custom was to pray with every family on whom he called in his wide journeyings, and if, as sometimes happened, he spent more days than one in some hospitable dwelling, he was wont to have household prayer as often as there were household meals, and to allow no visitor to come or go without asking, on his knees, that God would bless him. Besides an unknown number of camp-meetings and quarterly-meetings, this venerable man attended and presided over seven Conferences, widely separate, every year; and during the same space of time wrote to his preachers and friends upon an average about one thousand letters. For this enormous service his episcopal salary was sixty-four dollars yearly and his traveling expenses!

"Early educational advantages he had none. Most of his life was spent on horseback, in extemporized pulpits, or in log-cabins crowded with talking men and noisy women, bawling children and barking dogs—cabins which he was obliged to make his offices and studies, and where, with benumbed fingers, frozen ink, impracticable pens, and rumpled paper, he had to write his sermons, his journals, and his letters. Not unfrequently did he, like others, suffer from the malaria of a new, uncultivated country, and had headaches, toothaches, chills, fevers, and sore throat for his companions; and yet, despite all this, Francis Asbury was by no means an unlettered man. He became proficient in Latin, Greek, and Hebrew, read the Scriptures in the tongues in which they were originally written, was acquainted with several branches of polite literature, kept abreast with the history of his times, and although not an orator, was a dignified, eloquent, and impressive preacher. Thin, tall, and remarkably clean and neat, in a plain drab frock-coat, waistcoat, and breeches, a neat stock, and a broad-brimmed hat, this first and greatest Methodist American Bishop rode on horseback till he could ride no longer, and then he might often be seen hopping on crutches and helped in and out of his light spring-wagon as he still pursued his wide episcopal wanderings. Thus lived Francis Asbury until, in 1816, at the age of three-score years and ten, he died, and was followed to his grave in Baltimore by about twenty-five thousand of his friends. Before his death he solemnly enjoined that no life of him should be published, and that injunction has been substantially observed to the present; but if the reader wishes to see his monument, we invite him to step within the living walls of the present Methodist Episcopal Church of America, and there, while surveying the grand edifice of spiritual order and beauty, we ask him, as the inquirer in St. Paul's Cathedral is asked, to 'look around.'"

Such men were some of the early Methodists.

Let us close this chapter with Mr. Wesley's defini-
nition of what a Methodist is:

"A Methodist is one who has the love of God
shed abroad in his heart by the Holy Spirit given
unto him; one who loves the Lord his God with
all his heart and soul and mind and strength. He
rejoices evermore, prays without ceasing, and in
every thing gives thanks. His heart is full of love
to all mankind, and is purified from envy, malice,
wrath, and every unkind affection. His own desire,
and the one desire of his life, is not to do his own
will, but the will of Him that sent him. He keeps
all God's commandments, from the least to the
greatest. He follows not the customs of the world,
for vice does not lose its nature through its becoming fashionable. He fares not sumptuously every
day. He cannot lay up treasure upon earth, nor
can he adorn himself with gold or costly apparel.
He cannot join in any diversion that has the least
tendency to vice. He cannot speak evil of his
neighbor any more than he can tell a lie. He cannot utter unkind or evil words. No corrupt communication ever comes out of his mouth. He does
good unto all men — unto neighbors, strangers,
friends, and enemies. These are the marks of a
true Methodist." May we not say of a true Bible
Christian, of the highest type, of the loftiest personal attainments?

Are *these* the marks of a true Methodist?

Let each one ask his conscience the earnest question, "Am *I* a *true* Methodist?"

⇢ CHAPTER XV. ⇠

ONE hundred years have passed since the United States of America walked out into the blazing light of liberty—a free, independent nation, acknowledged to be such by her parent country, who for long years had tried in vain to keep her in obedient subjection.

One hundred years have passed since the Methodist Church was first organized within the boundaries of this New World, and, with its fresh, vigorous ecclesiasticism, started out hand in hand with the new, strong political power, it might be said, like young Samson not knowing the capabilities which lay in their unshorn locks.

One hundred years! And what do our eyes behold to-day? A country whose rapid growth is the marvel of the civilized world. Steadily westward has its "star of empire" gone till the thin stretch of colonies on the Atlantic coast has spread in teeming millions over the continent, and the waters of the Pacific lave city and village, vineyard and ranch, where are found population, wealth, and refinement equal to that of the oldest State whose face is turned to the rising sun. Steam and electricity have well-nigh annihilated time and space, and bound the remotest corners of the vast republic into quick access and sympathy with the whole. Commerce, agriculture, education, arts and sciences, flourish with ever-increasing prosperity; and yet we are but in our infancy.

In this centenary year of American Methodism for what may our grateful praise ascend? For a moment let us "stand still and see the salvation of God." In round numbers a membership of four million; twenty-six thousand itinerant and thirty-four thousand local preachers; near three hundred institutions of learning, from male and female classical seminaries to handsomely endowed and equipped universities; liberal contributions to every cause that advances the good of mankind; devoted missionaries in almost every land. And yet we have just begun to grapple with the powers of darkness.

The last quarter of a century has been signally productive of missionary zeal and enterprise. Long-closed doors have been opened unexpectedly —providentially. The Macedonian cry is heard on every breeze, and is being answered as never before. Still, only the seed is being sown. "What shall the harvest be" when the mighty tree is grown, when the abundant foliage comes forth, those leaves which are for "the healing of the nations?" Even now the "harvest is great, but the laborers are few." O let every heart, when special efforts are being made in this behalf this centenary year, add to our offerings earnest prayers to the "Lord of the harvest" that he send forth the much-needed laborers. If this petition comes from the depth of honest hearts, supplemented by the personal, supreme inquiry, "Lord, what wilt thou have *me* to do?" perchance the answer may come directly: "Go thy way; for *thou* art a chosen vessel unto me, to bear my name before the Gentiles." We exclaim with adoring wonder, "What hath God wrought!" Is he not the same "yesterday, to-day, and forever?" Looking back upon the great work accomplished in the past century, and remembering that "the unseen is greater far than that which appears," let us have faith that "to-morrow shall be as this day, and *much more abundant.*"

In that beautiful city which Oglethorpe founded, and where Whitefield and Wesley preached, their memories are cherished with tender reverence; while throughout the whole State—appropriately called the "Empire State of the South"—affection and respect are felt for them, it is in Savannah that their names are oftenest spoken. The city is one entire monument to its founder. To Whitefield's memory no marble shaft arises, nor needs he one. Bethesda, the "house of mercy" he founded one hundred and thirty-four years ago, still remains. True, the flames had twice destroyed the buildings,

and for a series of years the enterprise appeared
forever ended; but not thus was all the labor, the
devotion, the success of that good man to be forgotten.   In 1854 the board of managers of the Union
Society of Savannah, Georgia, bought a portion of
the original tract, and on the exact spot where
Whitefield's orphanage once stood was erected a
home for the friendless boys under their care.

The college for which Whitefield worked was
never carried into successful operation; but more
noble was the charity that fed, clothed, and housed
the destitute little creatures who there found a
home.   Two thousand boys have passed its portals
—going forth into the world to fight its battles,
armed with sound principles and habits of virtue
and industry.   Many more will doubtless share
its benefits, for its officers are men of high character and great benevolence, and time and labor are
bestowed upon its interests with no chary hand.
Annual celebrations are held, and are occasions of
great pleasure not only to the visitors from the city
and neighborhood, but to the young beneficiaries,
who are taught by the presence of sympathizing
friends, by cordial smiles and hand-clasps, by the
generous banquet, by garlands of beauty and ever-
green mottoes, by words of encouragement and inspiration from the orator of the day, that they are
expected to worthily fill their place in life; the
character of their original founder being held up

to them as worthy of all imitation. So, though
"being dead," Whitefield "yet speaketh," and his
spirit of love still hovers over this his once favorite spot.

To Mr. Wesley also a noble monument appears.
Not only with the silent eloquence of art does it bring
to mind the virtues and worth of the deceased, and
feelingly indicate the appreciation of the living,
but when day after day the walls of the Wesley
Monumental Church are vocal with the truths once
proclaimed by him for whom this majestic pile is
named, when from season to season penitents are
made to rejoice in the knowledge of the forgiveness
of their sins, and the praises of happy souls ascend in the hymns of the sweet singer in Israel—
Rev. Charles Wesley—then do these immortal utterances echo and reëcho in our hearts: "I look
upon the whole world as my parish"—simple, devoted words of John Wesley, prophetic in the realization of their extent; and then his brother's eloquent verity: "God buries his workmen, but carries
on his work;" till like a sweet refrain we hear, "The
best of all is, God is with us." It is well to em-
balm in never-ceasing fragrance words like these,
immortal in their truth; it is well to pay finest,
loftiest tribute to the good and true; it is well,
though "recognition and vindication may come
late, to have it come at last." So truly well, truly
fitting was it that in England's magnificent recep-

15

tacle for acknowledgments to her grandest, worthiest sons should, within a few years past, be placed a monument to the Reverends John and Charles Wesley. Most beautiful, most suggestive, and most gratifying the fact that the Dean of Westminster himself should unveil the memorial marble, and in words of simple truth and unaffected candor express the "obligation which the Church of England itself and which the Church of Christ owe to the labors of John and Charles Wesley," concluding by addressing the Non-conformist and Wesleyan ministers present, and invoking them to give him their "sympathy and coöperation in carrying on the work of promoting charity and good feeling and generous appreciation among the different branches of our divided Christendom." O lovely words of charity and brotherly kindness! How must the glorified spirits of those brothers, who once so labored for the advancement of the gospel of love and peace, have rejoiced at their utterance! So also must the angels have felt, those angels who first proclaimed the gospel with the sweetest words that up to that hour had ever greeted human ears: "Glory to God in the highest, and on earth peace, good-will toward men;" while God, who is love, must have been well pleased to hear. It is such episodes as these that gladden the heart when weary, not only with the "contradiction of sinners," but of saints the exclamation is wrung forth: "How long,

O Lord, before all brethren shall dwell together in unity?" Can we hope for its perfect consummation before the millennial dawn? As we glance back toward the ages gone we see that some of the purest, gentlest, and best have sometimes offended against the sweet spirit of love which generally ruled their breast. Between Paul and Barnabas the "contention was so sharp" that their paths were severed for awhile; the loving John, we are told in the short space of one chapter, wished to command fire from heaven to consume the inhospitable Samaritans, and forbade one who cast out devils in the Master's name, because he followed not with them; Luther and Zwingli held bitter controversies; Wesley and Whitefield allowed their opposite religious views to alienate them for a little time. These prominent instances we may take for our comfort. *Wherefore?* Because each one shows —as does every example in God's book of a deviation from the perfect law of love and obedience— after experiences of penitence and humility, of vows renewed, and a better life. What more candid acknowledgment could be desired than Paul's injunction to "take Mark and bring him with thee, for he is profitable to me for the ministry"—the very Mark whose former instability was the subject of variance between Paul and Barnabas. When Jesus replied to John, "Forbid him not, for he that is not against us is for us," could the lesson ever be needed by him again? and should not all Christ's disciples heed its teachings till time's latest period? And O when, with a look of sorrow mingled with displeasure—harder for John to endure than the mere words of the rebuke—Jesus said to him, "Ye know not what manner of spirit ye are of," can we doubt that in the revolution of feeling it caused his heart went forth to those Samaritans, upon whom his anger had so recently rested, with a pitying compassion akin to his Master's when he beheld Jerusalem and wept over it? O thank God for a compassionate, forgiving Saviour—for the declaration that "this man receiveth sinners," first uttered in contemptuous scorn, but now and for ages past the comfort and reliance of aching, trusting hearts. Thank God, above all things, for the assertion of that central truth of the Bible, of the hope in time and glory in eternity—that "God is love." Now, know we that for all variations from his perfect law of love we, his weak disciples here, can—as did the hosts that have already "crossed the flood"—find supplies in the inexhaustible fullness of Him who has said: "I have loved thee with an everlasting love; therefore, with loving-kindness have I drawn thee." Yes; love is surely the last, best, and highest analysis of the gospel. Then, let Christians take for their watch-word this precious benediction: "Grace be with all them that love our Lord Jesus Christ in sincerity." Whether they claim it as a personal, direct blessing on their own souls or a broad expression of fervent Christian charity, in either case shall love be brought into purer, more active exercise. If we were granted but one verse out of the Holy Scriptures on which to stay our human needs; if out of that vast treasury we were allowed to select but one jewel; if but one declaration was given to us by which to live and by which to die—it should be that sublimest revelation of Scripture: "For God *so loved* the world that he gave his only-begotten Son, that *whosoever* believeth in him should not perish, but have everlasting life." This one glorious word of God is enough for time; it is enough for eternity Even those countless cycles can never exhaust the theme. We can only exclaim:

> Through all eternity to thee
> A grateful song I'll raise;
> But O! eternity's too short
> To utter all thy praise.

"Glory be to the Father, and to the Son, and to the Holy Ghost, as it was in the beginning. is now, and ever shall be, world without end. Amen."

THE END.

www.ingramcontent.com/pod-product-compliance
Lightning Source LLC
Chambersburg PA
CBHW030108030726
47498CB00007B/2301